Tulsa's
A story of Greenwood Oklahoma

Tulsa's Black Wall Street
A story of Greenwood Oklahoma

Author's Note

This book is a work of fiction. Any reference to actual events, real people, living or dead, or to real locales are intended only to give the book a sense of reality and authenticity. Other names, characters, places and incidents are a product of the author's imagination or are used fictitiously. Any resemblance in actual persons, living or dead, business establishments, agencies, events or locales is entirely coincidental.

Tulsa's Black Wall Street

A story of Greenwood Oklahoma

Dedication

Based on a true event, this book is dedicated to the memory of Greenwood Oklahoma. In defiance of an openly oppressive society filled with hate, racism and bigotry the black residents of Greenwood prospered. Facing obstacles that were extreme, these black men and women refused to stop fighting for what was right or to take their eyes off of their goals. Researching this story and discovering how events unfolded was painful to me. Despite an exhaustive research, I will never really know these people but I do understand them and learned from their experience. I learned from their story that life will give us obstacles and these deterrents may be unfair or extreme. But we are also given choices in life. Break through the obstacles or let the obstacles break you. Obstacles in our way shouldn't be seen as automatically meant to stop us. Hurdles should be viewed as pointing the way to a new route, new possibilities, and new doorways.

I dedicate this book to the brave black men and women of Greenwood and thank them for holding tight to their dreams of a better tomorrow. Thank you.

Tulsa's Black Wall Street
A story of Greenwood Oklahoma

And a special dedication to….Willie Weathers.

Tulsa's Black Wall Street

A story of Greenwood Oklahoma

Tulsa's Black Wall Street

A story of Greenwood Oklahoma

Chapter 1

It would qualify as an absolutely perfect lazy early summer day. The location was a small rural settlement in Oklahoma, near the banks of the Arkansas River. It was a community called Tulsa and the year was 1908. A light blue sky shined brilliantly as the countryside was bathed in brilliant summer sunlight. In a picture perfect setting, white and pink clover grew on the hillsides as cows grazed contently in the meadows. A soft breeze blew through the trees while birds sang and crickets chirped. The joyful sound of children's screams could be heard echoing throughout the woods as they frolicked. Past the cow pasture, through the trees and down a narrow path, six young children were romping and excitedly having fun. The six friends were Kenny (Junior) Chase, Henry Fletcher, Emma Burns, Joseph Burns, Ezekiel (Easy) White and Chitto (CT) Red Eagle. Nothing could be better they thought, than running around, playing hide "n" seek, splashing water and swimming in the local creek. Worley's Creek was remote with grassy shallow banks and lined with a colorful variety of trees. The air was rich with fragrances of pine and flowering dogwood.

Tulsa's Black Wall Street

A story of Greenwood Oklahoma

The creek was crystal clear and a sound of running water offered a relaxing hypnotic type quality. As they swam, the water seemed to magically drink away the heat from their bodies. While enjoying the creek they found themselves completely absorbed in their fun. They were carefree and unconcerned about the passage of time or worries of the grown-up world.

Standing in the tree line was a man silently taking in the children's activity. A cruel sneer formed on his unshaven pot marked face as he leaned forward, eyes bearing straight ahead. His face grew increasingly rigid, jaws clamped tight, teeth grinding and the veins in his neck seemed waiting to explode. The man held back his anger as long as he could, but he was now totally consumed by hate. A burning rage hissed through his body like deadly poison and it demanded release. His mouth was slightly open and a glisten of snot dribbled above his cracked lips as the wrath of hate consumed him. Suddenly the children's tranquility was shattered as the man erupted like a volcano and began screeching violently. Kenny's father, Kenneth Sr. stepped from the tree line and angrily snapped "JUNIOR!!!!"

Tulsa's Black Wall Street

A story of Greenwood Oklahoma

Infuriated, Kenneth Sr. roughly grabbed Junior by the left arm and whirled him around. Kenneth Sr. then began poking Junior in his chest. As he easily man handled Junior the old man kept asking "What the hell are you doing here with these niggers", referring to Easy and CT.

Junior's attempts to explain that CT was an Indian and Easy was CT's first cousin was pointless. Junior even tried to temper the situation by reminding his father that Easy had saved him from drowning at that same creek nearly a year ago. But every time Junior opened his mouth Kenneth Sr. only got angrier. Every word from Junior only served to fuel the fire of hate that burned inside of his father. Each utterance was like tossing gasoline on an already raging fire. The old man's face was now red and knuckles white from clenching Junior's arm too hard. Dragging Junior away from the creek Kenneth Sr. exploded in a ferocious wave of verbal assaults. As his primeval instinct took over, Kenneth Sr. screamed at Junior. "Dammit, mingling with those niggers is destructive to the boundaries of loyalty to our white race. White people and niggers are a different and unequal species. It is an affront to God's law and spelled out in the bible's Old Testament. The curse of Ham as told in Genesis 9 makes it clear.

Tulsa's Black Wall Street

A story of Greenwood Oklahoma

Niggers were designated inferior to white people as God's righteous punishment for their sins. They were separated from the white man by color, superior mental and moral traits. Speaking of that Injun, hell boy an Injun ain't nothing but a nigger with straight hair. I would have rather that you had drowned last year than be indebted to a nigger."

Kenneth Sr. bent Junior's arm back while punching him in the stomach and forced him along the path. Junior made the error of attempting to block his father's punch to the stomach. A fire of fury and hatred erupted as his father whirled Junior around to land a solid blow on his jaw, right below his eye. As the old man spewed hatred, his words stung Junior nearly as much as the blow. However Junior just gritted his teeth and remained silent. He and his father crossed the field to finally reach the wagon. Grabbing the reins and with a "Giddy-yup mule", they rode away. The other children just stood there, by the creek, with a blank look in their eyes as they stared in horror. They desperately searched their minds for something to say and to make sense of what they had witnessed.

Words failed them and their hearts fell silent as they stood there momentarily stunned.

Tulsa's Black Wall Street

A story of Greenwood Oklahoma

Internally Easy and CT burned with anger as they would frequently encounter similar racist mentalities. They looked at each other knowingly, thinking to themselves, "what the hell?" Almost in sync, they simultaneously turned their attention to search the eyes of the other children waiting for some type of reaction or response. The other children genuinely liked Easy and CT. Mr. Chase's comments resulted in an awkward situation for the other children. They desperately searched their minds for something reasonable to say. Their struggle was like trying to floss with barbed wire. Clearly uncomfortable, Emily broke the silence by finally saying, "Come on everybody. Let's just get out of here." Joseph agreed by saying, "Um, yeah. Let's leave before Mr. Chase decides to come back with friends."

Joseph and Emily Burns were siblings and their father's land bordered Easy's family farm. Easy performed occasional farm tasks working for their father to include planting and harvesting. Easy's family were black land owners who had owned their own farm for nearly fifty years. Beginning in the 1820's, the U.S. Government forced Five Civilized Tribes east of the Mississippi River to leave their lands. The Five Civilized Tribes were: Chickasaws, Choctaws, Cherokees, Creeks, and Seminoles.

Tulsa's Black Wall Street
A story of Greenwood Oklahoma

In mid-winter these Tribes were forcibly marched and resettled into new lands over the infamous "Trail of Tears." Described as "the dead and hopeless home of souls", Tulsa began as an outpost of the Creek Indians. As a boy Samson White, Easy's grandfather escaped slavery by running away from a Texas plantation in the 1830's. He made his way to this Indian Territory seeking refuge from the Creek settlements. The Indian community adopted young Samson and incorporated him into their settlement. He was allowed to live freely in the Oklahoma Indian Territory. As a free person Samson ultimately married a Creek woman, acquired a position of authority and property. Samson raised seven children and the land was passed down to his children. Samson's eldest son was Hezekiah White. Similar to his father, Hezekiah also married a Creek, gaining more property and remained in the territory to raise a family.

Much like his father and in-laws Hezekiah continued traditional activities of hunting and subsistence agriculture. But, the region of his birth and designated as Indian Territory would become Oklahoma. After the Civil War, U.S. Indian treaties provided for slave liberation and land allotments ranging from 40 to100 acres.

Tulsa's Black Wall Street

A story of Greenwood Oklahoma

The land would be granted to the newly freed blacks to assist in the economic transition away from slavery. Word of mouth spread quickly and freed slaves headed for the Oklahoma territory in mass.

The Indian nation opened their arms to freed slaves from all across the country. Oklahoma boasted of having more all-Black towns and communities than any other state in the land, and these communities opened their arms to other blacks. Seeking greater opportunities after the civil war, by the late 1880s there was great political pressure by some displayed southerners to open Oklahoma and allow white settlement. Discouraged by existing economic conditions after the civil war, some poor whites migrated to Oklahoma. They traveled by wagons, horses, trains, and even on foot for the chance to start over. These whites saw the abundance of land and natural resources as an ideal circumstance for their prosperity. They firmly believed that availability of property rights to everyone in the Indian Territory was inevitable. Some found suitable plots and Indians did not always discourage these whites from squatting. However to these white squatters disappointment, despite settling, the Five Civilized Tribes retained sovereignty.

Tulsa's Black Wall Street
A story of Greenwood Oklahoma

The white squatters were quickly made aware that they could not own land or vote. Despite Indian sovereignty, whites continued their steady stream into the land of abundant resources. The whites came in two categories; very rich and very poor. Because of their inability to own land whites complained of perceived mistreatment and an inadequate justice system. Whites continued to follow party politics and attended national conventions, because they believed that Indian Territory offered potential. Indians had lived on this land for many years, growing crops, raising families, and developing their own culture. Responding to white demands, in 1889 President Benjamin Harrison bowed to political pressure making the first of a series of authorizations.

The years between 1900 and 1906 encompassed massive white settlement. Whites largely from the south obtained large swaths of land, previously designated specifically to Indian tribes. As whites rapidly moved into Indian Territory, Oklahoma was spreading out and filling in. In 1905 the discovery of oil prompted a rush of entrepreneurs to the area. Tulsa's population immediately began to swell.

Tulsa's Black Wall Street

A story of Greenwood Oklahoma

Unlike earlier settlers, primarily from the south, most of the newer settlers were from the commercial centers of the east coast and lower mid-west. This migration drastically changed the territory's demographics. By the year 1906, whites outnumbered American Indians by a ratio of 6 to 1.

Unfortunately, the changing demographics and new local political structure reinforced by federal government policy aided whites in their pursuit of land. The government's efforts made it easy for unethical whites to separate less sophisticated Indians from their individual land holdings. Homesteads and town sites created through the government's legal maneuvering eventually wrestled most of assigned Indian Territory from Indian control. Wealthy white settlers took full advantage of the situation. Efforts by local governments with the aid of prominent politicians also resulted in President Roosevelt establishing Oklahoma as the 46th state in November 1907. Easy, CT and their families were born in Oklahoma. CT's mother was Hezekiah's sister (Sehoy Red Eagle). She and her husband (Chebona Bula Red Eagle) each had inherited land from their respective parents and their land had been in the family for multiple generations.

Tulsa's Black Wall Street

A story of Greenwood Oklahoma

The white children had relocated to Oklahoma with their families only in the past 10 years. Many of the new settlers, like Kenneth Sr., were former slaveholders. Black land owners were unheard of at that time, especially for southern whites. The arrangement of a black land owning neighbor proved to be exceptionally challenging and resulted in uneasiness for some of Hezekiah's white neighbors. A lot of these whites had very little respect for Indians. They had even less respect for blacks, regarding them as mentally inferior, physically and culturally unevolved, and apelike in appearance. These whites liked to think of themselves as hard-working and moral people made in the image of God. On the other hand, they had stereotyped blacks as lazy, ignorant, uncivilized and cursed by God to be subservient.

The fact that Easy's family owned land was seen as an abomination by some whites in the community especially Kenneth Chase Sr. These white people believed the superior position was assigned to the white race. To complicate matters, they had also been deluded to believe slaves were truly content in bondage. After all they were all given food, clothing and a place to stay. Kenneth Sr. would often brag how he gave his niggers extra molasses and the day off for Christmas.

Tulsa's Black Wall Street

A story of Greenwood Oklahoma

He was proud of the fact that he "seldom" beat them; only when they deserved it. Living together with blacks on terms of social and political equality was contrary to the core beliefs of these former southerners. As it turned out Hezekiah White was a principled man who did not hesitate to assert his independence.

Carefully spoken and without drama, when he spoke his words had an air of finality to them. He lived by the old Indian order, loved his brethren and fervently believed in a strong family bond. Born free in the Oklahoma Indian Territory, before it was granted statehood, he was a proud native. Hezekiah had heard all the stories about slavery's brutality from his grandfather. He was told to always bear in mind how whites had oppressed, tortured and denied freedom to blacks by enslavement. Over the years Hezekiah had encountered numerous runaway slaves escaping from the border states of Arkansas and Texas. He had heard their stories of slavery's cruelty first hand. He had grown to believe that white people were an inwardly depraved people by nature. From birth he was taught by his Creek family that no legacy was as rich as honesty.

Tulsa's Black Wall Street

A story of Greenwood Oklahoma

The influence of the Creek Nation on the lives of Hezekiah and his family could not be measured when it came to honesty, integrity and moral courage. He understood their exploitative nature and could easily see the deceitful intent of whites relocating to the Indian Territory. Hezekiah feared that his people's sense of fairness in dealing with whites would not be reciprocated and would ultimately be the cause of harm or damage to the Indian Nation as he knew it. That was not to say that all whites were deemed untrustworthy, but he felt decision makers in the white government had been tainted by people with evil intent. He believed their intentions were to steal, corrupt and gain wealth at the expense of the Indians. Hezekiah relished his freedom.

He also loved his Indian relatives and relationship with the Creek nation. He was not hesitant to flaunt his status as a proud land owner in the presence of whites. Hezekiah understood the ambivalence of white people and all about their well-documented injustices during slavery. He was determined not to give up on his dreams for anything and was not intimidated as shown by his outspoken nature. For southern whites Hezekiah's straightforward language and manner was hard to take.

Tulsa's Black Wall Street
A story of Greenwood Oklahoma

Hezekiah challenged the stereotypical attitude that whites wanted portrayed and this presented a problems if other blacks followed his lead.

Tulsa's Black Wall Street

A story of Greenwood Oklahoma

Chapter 2

America's search for oil prompted a rush of entrepreneurs, speculators, and wildcatters to seek their fortunes on the great Indian plains. The discovery of oil in 1905 resulted in an overwhelming demand for labor. At the time of statehood Oklahoma was known as the Oil Capital of the World. By the time President Roosevelt established Oklahoma as the 46th state it produced most of the oil in the United States. Although agriculture remained the dominant economic activity in the state, its relative role was much diminished. Pay for working in the oil fields was so lucrative that workers were irresistibly attracted to work. Workers left farms in mass to capitalize on the high pay. The work was physically demanding but no more so than the farm labor they were leaving. Profits from the oil industry helped Oklahoma's economy fare better than most in the United States. This was a period of significant productivity increases, sales increases, wage increases and rising demand. The rapidly growing economy was also spurred by railroad construction, expansion of timber harvesting and coal mining.

Tulsa's Black Wall Street

A story of Greenwood Oklahoma

The quickly expanding increase in the amount of goods and services resulted in economic boom for both whites as well as blacks. For a time, a fluid social relationship existed between blacks and whites despite the recent history of slavery.

With an abundance of work positions available, black workers began to compete for jobs usually reserved for whites. A sizeable portion of blacks energetically began buying land and establishing their own businesses. The growing economic success of blacks did not go unnoticed, creating outrage among reactionary forces such as the Ku Klux Klan. Of particular concern to the Ku Klux Klan was a black man named O.W. Gurley. Gurley was a well-off black land-proprietor from Arkansas. As a business visionary he resigned from a presidential appointment under President Grover Cleveland to strike out alone. With an interest in the Oklahoma Land speculation, by a development of events chance, Mr. Gurley met Hezekiah White. With similar business acumen and a firm belief in the unalienable rights of blacks, the two of them immediately became fast friends.

Tulsa's Black Wall Street
A story of Greenwood Oklahoma

Aided by Hezekiah, in 1906 O.W. Gurley purchased 40 acres of land that was designated to be sold to colored people only. Among Gurley's first businesses was a rooming house which was located on a dusty trail near the railroad tracks. This road was given the name Greenwood Avenue, named after a city in Mississippi. The area became very popular among black migrants who were fleeing oppression. Surrounded by likeminded freed men, blacks found refuge on Greenwood Avenue. Adding to the rooming house, Gurley went on to build three two-story buildings and five residential homes. He also purchased an 80-acre farm in nearby Rogers County. White people began to feel threatened. An irrational fear of possible black independence, economic and political influence fostered an atmosphere of concern among whites. With Kenneth Sr. leading the charge, white supremacists began forming political and social groups. The sole purpose of these groups was to promote the rights of white people and conversely keep blacks in their rightful station. These whites believed they were superior to blacks and perceived the mere act of competing for jobs was a degradation of the unwritten etiquette of race relations (or Jim Crow).

Tulsa's Black Wall Street

A story of Greenwood Oklahoma

White racial intolerance led to the occasional violent attacks and lynching of blacks.

Showing their rage over the new social arrangement, these white supremacists targeted local elected officials. In demanding change, white people cast themselves in a light as victims and asserted non-whites deserved maltreatment. The pressure placed on these officials via a concerted effort proved successful. These elected officials, who were also neighbors, business associates, church and family members of the white supremacists ultimately bowed to the pressure. Officials promptly enacted local laws meant to disenfranchise non-whites and codify inequality. Tulsa passed an ordinance that mandated residential segregation by forbidding blacks or whites from residing on any block where three-fourths or more of the residents were of the other race. City leaders next established and implemented segregated "colored" boundaries based on Greenwood Avenue. This street location was important in the decision process because it ran north for over a mile from the Frisco Railroad yards, and it was one of the few streets that did not cross between both black and white neighborhoods.

Tulsa's Black Wall Street
A story of Greenwood Oklahoma

It was determined that colored boundaries were from Pine Street to the North, Archer Street and the Frisco tracks to the South, Cincinnati Street on the West, and Lansing Street on the East. Because it was centered on Greenwood Avenue, the colored part of town was labeled Greenwood. However a number of city officials and white residents callously called the area Little Africa. By law, public facilities and government services were divided into separate "white" and "colored" domains. Characteristically, public domains for non-whites were underfunded and of inferior quality. City officials also passed laws that made voter registration more restrictive, essentially forcing some non-white voters off of voting rolls. They verbally rubber stamped economic oppression by agreeing to look the other way in allowing employment discrimination thereby denying non-whites economic opportunities. They defended implementing these segregated measures and Jim Crow as a means of ensuring racial peace. Blacks and Indians saw the measures for what they were, a function of racism with the intent to dehumanize non-whites.

The Tulsa black community was very active religiously. City officials sought out one of the most notable church leaders to act as an intermediary.

Tulsa's Black Wall Street

A story of Greenwood Oklahoma

The man they contacted was Reverend Sam Stubbs, pastor of Vernon AME Church. They requested his help in coordinating a meeting with the right people in the black community. The meeting's purpose was to deliver the new policies that had been implemented verbally and first hand. It was only fifty years post slavery and these officials understood that a number of freedmen were still illiterate. At the start of the gathering, city officials began by extolling their Christian values. In a patronizing manner they fashioned themselves as beleaguered defenders of traditional American values. Arrogantly they told attendees how people of different races often prefer to live with their own kind. In laying out the new Jim Crow policies, they stated further that social separation of whites and non-whites was a regional custom. By the United States constitution they were free to legally regulate their own social affairs. Continuing they assured everyone that Tulsa's city leaders only concern was for the welfare of their colored population. With a sardonic grin on his face the Mayor stood to assure everyone that segregation was not harmful to anyone. Similarly he was confident that their position on segregation was God's position.

To those in attendance the message was received as dismissive, divisive and condescending.

Tulsa's Black Wall Street
A story of Greenwood Oklahoma

Hezekiah was sitting next to O.W. at the meeting. Hezekiah's knuckles were almost white from clenching his fist too hard. He gritted his teeth hard in an effort to remain silent. His face grew red with suppressed rage. O.W. placed a hand on Hezekiah's shoulder in an effort to calm him.

Immediately after concluding their message, the city officials departed. Recognizing a state of great uneasiness in attendees, Reverend Stubbs took to the pulpit. In a calm manner he advocated restraint in requesting that everyone retain their composure. He stressed that solutions did appear complicated, but blacks must be the people of better natures. The Reverend proposed working with an open heart and assured the Lord would make a way. He asked that as Jesus did, they must love without prejudice. He followed by saying, "I beg you to resist the call for hate. Use your higher mind and the emotions that bring a sense of love; for with evocation of such love comes bravery, nobility and the right kind of pride. When in life we hurt another, we hurt ourselves also. When we love another it is a healing for both, for how else do we know ourselves but through our own actions? When our actions reflect the truth of our souls, social justice will be demanded by all. We must pray on this."

Tulsa's Black Wall Street

A story of Greenwood Oklahoma

Every time one of the so called leaders opened their mouth Hezekiah got angrier. To Hezekiah every word stung and it was like pouring fuel on the fire that burned inside of him. At first Hezekiah was going to swallow any retort, smile and move on. However the racist actions and superior demeanor of Tulsa's leaders was infuriating. After all Hezekiah was likely more wealthy than most of his neighbors and the city's leaders as well. His family owned considerable land, building up their farms with hard work and determination. He hadn't meant to wind himself up so much but his rage finally consumed him. He felt a swelling of the veins rushing blood to his head seemingly waiting to explode. Hezekiah did not wish to speak out of term or be disrespectful by saying things that probably better left unsaid, but he snapped. Forcefully he said, "Reverend Stubbs we own land and we pay taxes. I know how whites have always lied and broken treaties with Indians. They have gone to war rather than free colored people from the brutality of slavery. Why should we believe or trust what they say now? As a people we must think of our children and our children's children.

Do they think white people have genuine concern for us or our children?

Tulsa's Black Wall Street
A story of Greenwood Oklahoma

If we lie down for this, just like in slavery, white people will feel they have the right to control every aspect of our lives. There comes a time when a man must stand-up and fight. Them crackers are riled about our independence and mean all non-whites no good. Our dark skin is not a badge of shame. If we don't stop this now, it will not be good for us down the road. No disrespect Pastor, but their mouth is no bible and we don't need prayer, we need guns."

Reverend Stubbs winced as some in the crowd shouted in agreement with Hezekiah. After some thought O.W. stood and walked to the front of the church. After looking over the assembled crowd he asked Reverend Stubbs for permission to speak. After requesting silence, he cleared his throat and began. "It is my belief that there is a lot of truth in what my friend Hezekiah White says. I agree with Hezekiah that their motives are not in our best interest and as a people we must not lose focus. Our actions will affect generations to come so we must think of our children and our children's children. As much as I agree with Hezekiah I don't think violence is the solution. It is not our right to punish one for thinking as he does, no matter how much we disagree. " He paused briefly, looked at Hezekiah to say "My friend, I may disagree with you, but I am not against you."

Tulsa's Black Wall Street

A story of Greenwood Oklahoma

Returning his attention to the crowd, he continued "Tulsa's actions are in fact a signal of bad faith. I hate what Tulsa's leaders are trying to do. What they are trying to do is wrong. However I want to address the wrong as a responsible citizen not a colored citizen. A responsible citizen is the one that sees something wrong in the community, something he is not satisfied with or, that he cannot agree with and responds. We don't respond by blaming those leaders but by designing ways and means of bringing a solution to the issue at hand." O.W. spoke softly, but he was sincere and the crowd was hanging on his every word. From the body language of each person, he also appeared to be saying exactly the right thing. Carrying on O.W. said, "Let me shine some light on this situation for you. It is not unusual for fear to be the first reaction of adversity, it's normal. However it is whites who should fear us. We don't need white's permission to act as one family in all our ethnicities and faiths. If you think you can do a thing or think you can't do a thing, you're right.

I believe we as a people have a better chance of economic progress if we pool our resources, work together and support each other's businesses. They wish to separate, so let them separate our money as well.

Tulsa's Black Wall Street

A story of Greenwood Oklahoma

The money we normally pay them for goods and services, we will keep in Greenwood. This will mean less money for their businesses and reduce their income. Less business also means they will need fewer employees. But the foundation is self-determination and dedication to a dream. As a people we must have the will to truly choose our own path. We can one day and soon, aspire to be what we are destined to be and that is...together." The crowd was transfixed in the moment; motivated by O.W's thoughts. His suggestions struck a tone with the crowd as their eyes seem to light up. It was like hundreds of ideas were streaming through their collective brains. The crowd had heard something new, something amazing they wanted to be a part of it and grew excited.

Another black American entrepreneur, J.B. (John the Baptist) Stradford, also in attendance was similarly inspired by O.W.'s remarks. J.B. Stradford was a former Kentucky slave who was not afraid to preach the gospel of equal treatment and racial solidarity for black Americans. College-educated in Ohio at Oberlin College, Stradford received his law degree from Indiana University. Before Tulsa became his destiny, J.B. was practicing as a lawyer in Indianapolis and yearning to influence black equality.

Tulsa's Black Wall Street

A story of Greenwood Oklahoma

He took inspiration from O.W.'s appeal to racial pride and the level of receptive excitement in the audience. He stood, unbuttoned his suit jacket and straightened his white shirt before speaking up in support of O.W. "Our white visitors have had a lot of words to say tonight and so has my friend O.W. There is a funny thing about words. Words can build you up, or they can tear you down. I beg of you to not let the white man's words tear you down or dampen your spirit. O.W. is correct in his line of thinking. The two most powerful words in the world are I believe. If you say I believe out loud, you unleash extraordinary powers therefore we must be careful how we use these two words. If you say I believe that I am going to have a great day, it puts your life on track for an amazing day. On the other hand, if you say, I believe it's going to be a bad day; immediately the day grows gray and forbidding. We are Tulsa citizens, but whites don't want to recognize us. But we have the ability to make them.

Let me just say that I believe we have the potential to be a politically powerful, successful Negro-friendly community. Having said that, I also believe brother Hezekiah was correct. I am also in complete agreement that there is no need to bow down or be subservient to anyone white.

Tulsa's Black Wall Street
A story of Greenwood Oklahoma

I believe the time has come for us as a people and community to stand-up and fight. Instead of cowering and accommodating as the white man desires, by our actions we can provide hope to every Negro in America. I believe in our success and I am on board with this train. Just like O.W. I am willing to invest my last penny to see that our dreams of success become reality."

The church was momentarily quiet as what was just said had to sink in to the crowd. What came next was a deafening explosion of cheers. The crowd was electrified and the cheers were almost deafening. Everyone shouted, screamed, stomped their feet and gave every ounce of power in their lungs to show their support. Seeing all these successful likeminded men made the others want to emulate their success. Pastor Stubbs, Hezekiah White, O.W. Gurley and J.B. Stradford stood, as a group, in front of the church to a continued round of thunderous applause.

Tulsa's Black Wall Street
A story of Greenwood Oklahoma

Chapter 3

Black Tulsa or Greenwood began to take shape. Greenwood Avenue quickly grew into a black commercial district with many red brick buildings. These buildings belonged to black people and they were thriving businesses. With his prominence and wealth, O.W. Gurley purchased large tracts of real estate in the northeastern part of Tulsa, which he had subdivided and sold exclusively to other blacks. True to his word J. B. Stradford later built the Stradford Hotel in Greenwood, where blacks could enjoy the amenities of hotels who served only whites. It was said to be the largest black-owned hotel in the United States.

The area became home to several prominent black businessmen as the Greenwood community mobilized its resources. Greenwood boasted a variety of thriving businesses including hotels, law and doctor's offices, banks, cafes, newspapers, pharmacies, schools, libraries, grocery stores, movie theaters, barbershops and hair salons. Eventually there were hundreds of businesses, all were Black-owned and operated.

Tulsa's Black Wall Street

A story of Greenwood Oklahoma

Greenwood's progressive black community also contained a number of elegant houses belonging to doctors, lawyers and business owners. These expensive homes were built by black carpenters and well furnished by black merchants. The idea of black independence planted in the minds of those attending that church meeting, like flowers in a garden had blossomed. Greenwood was a tremendous success. The resolve of Tulsa's whites to keep blacks subservient and in their rightful place had gone terribly awry. Not only did blacks want to contribute to the success of their own shops, but there were segregation laws enacted by Tulsa officials that prevented them from shopping anywhere other than Greenwood. As intended by Tulsa's officials, blacks were not disenfranchised by the Greenwood boundary. On the contrary they embraced the boundaries, affectionately called their community Greenwood and prospered from it. By calling it Greenwood, many people considered Tulsa and Greenwood to be two separate cities rather than one city of united communities.

The citizens of Greenwood took pride in this fact because the community was of their own making. Additionally it was something they had all to themselves and did not have to share with the white community of Tulsa.

Tulsa's Black Wall Street

A story of Greenwood Oklahoma

However, this was only partially true because whites did voluntarily frequent the Greenwood section of Tulsa; or as they called it, Little Africa. The Stradford Hotel amenities and competitive pricing attracted the occasional white patron. Then there was also the Little Bell Café, famous for its smothered chicken and rice. The luncheon special was such a delicacy, that whites from Tulsa even put aside their racist attitudes to make it over to the café. The neighborhood also offered nightclubs for entertainment from late evening into the early hours of the morning. These nightclubs were quite popular with some white people offering a hotbed of jazz and blues. Greenwood even possessed its own black print media and did not have to rely on white newspapers.

The genius of Greenwood was that blacks pooled their resources, worked together and supported each other's businesses. As it turned out Greenwood's economy was much more stable and stronger than Tulsa's. Greenwood was one of the most affluent communities anywhere and it became known as "Negro Wall Street." Unfortunately for them in their effort to undermine Tulsa's black citizens, whites were victimized by the law of unintended consequences.

Tulsa's Black Wall Street
A story of Greenwood Oklahoma

Fortunately for blacks, there were two unexpected upsides to the segregation laws established by Tulsa's officials. First of all spending black dollars in the black community established a financially independent community. Secondly, white dollars earned by black Tulsans stayed in the community, giving Greenwood merchants the spoils of their white neighbors. Additionally segregation laws did not prohibit whites from patronizing black establishments; and patronizing Greenwood's merchants whites did. White patrons spending in Greenwood further drew from the Tulsa white merchant's economy. Black dollars invested in the Black community also produced self-pride, self-sufficiency, and self-determination. Blacks flocked to the thriving city to escape racial prejudice elsewhere.

Hezekiah was favorably impressed by the continued economic growth and social progress of Greenwood. Joining the long list of new business owners, Hezekiah and his sister's husband Chebona Bula Red Eagle purchased two buildings. The family rented one building that housed Johnson's Barber shop and pool hall. Hezekiah and his brother-in-law owned and operated a cigar store.

Tulsa's Black Wall Street

A story of Greenwood Oklahoma

Tobacco was one of the multiple crops raised by Hezekiah and Chebona Bula on their respective farms. The store was staffed by children and extended members of both families. Both men expected that their children and the following generations would benefit thereby making Oklahoma and the world a better place.

Life on the farm was hard but a special place that offered Hezekiah White self-sufficiency. For Easy and his siblings, performing the endless number of tasks, days were long and required a great deal of endurance. The family awoke each morning to the sound of a rooster crowing. Cows mooed contently in one corner of the farm and in the other corner came the squeals and snorts of fat pigs. Chickens lazily cackled around the coop and the horses grazed the meadow. Each day the children got up at the crack of dawn and worked till the sun set performing back breaking chores. Early mornings were sometimes their own reward. Every fragrance was fresh, like the page of a new book. The sun rose like a flower opening, gifting its petals unto the world. In the early morning light, birds would chirp an explicit melody; the morning air smelled of honeysuckle, dew was a silk over the garden, and the mountains were silhouettes against a crimson sky.

Tulsa's Black Wall Street

A story of Greenwood Oklahoma

Every morning, year round, after rising they would eat a small breakfast, cut wood, feed the horses, oxen, cattle, hogs, chickens and gather eggs. On the family farm Hezekiah kept enough animals for work and their own consumption. Anything excess they grew or raised was bartered with neighbors for whatever they could not grow themselves.

During the spring, in addition to daily chores there was plowing, planting and tending to crops. They planted wheat, tobacco, corn, green beans, potatoes, strawberries, watermelons, tomatoes and tended a fruit orchard. Hezekiah was fairly wealthy and owned both horses and oxen. Using these animals to plow the fields saved time and manpower making it easier to plant. The use of animals aided Easy as he sometimes contracted his services to neighboring farmers for extra money. He mostly aided a neighboring farmer named Sam Burns. Sam was the father of Emma and Joseph Burns, two of Easy's childhood friends. Aside from CT, these two were his closest friends all through childhood.

If lucky, on some days Easy would finish his work before sundown. This afforded him an opportunity to either go for a swim or fish.

Tulsa's Black Wall Street

A story of Greenwood Oklahoma

Some nights he would return home with a batch of freshly caught fish to cook. After supper, he would go to bed early so he could get a fresh start the following morning.

Spring was also a time of having a lot of baby animals on the farm. His mother began to dig meat out of the hay, where it was stored during the winter. His mother also had to purchase material for new dresses when his older sisters had outgrown some of their old spring and summer dresses. The girls did not wear winter dresses during summer because they were too hot. The smaller dresses were either passed down or made into quilts if they were in disrepair. Younger children also put their shoes up because they only wore them when the ground was too cold. By mid-summer the harvesting began. Easy and his family harvested wheat, tobacco and a variety of vegetables and fruits. Wheat and tobacco was harvested and sold as a source of income. The fruits and vegetables not consumed for daily sustenance were either canned to be eaten during winter months or bartered.

The years proved quite profitable for Hezekiah and time seemed to fly by. For his parents Easy turned 16 years old in what almost seemed like a blur.

Tulsa's Black Wall Street
A story of Greenwood Oklahoma

Easy was well built, about five feet eight inches tall, tipping the scales at approximately 160 pounds. There was no fat on his well-conditioned body. He'd filled out with muscle long before his peers and his voice broke before he was officially a teen. Over the years, bit by bit, Easy grew, changed and matured. He now looked like a slimmer reflection of Hezekiah. One summer afternoon, after completing his chores early, Hezekiah allowed Easy free time. Easy decided that he would head to Worley's creek to swim and cool off. Before making off, Easy invited his cousin CT to join him in grabbing a watermelon and going for a swim. CT had to carry a load of tobacco to the cigar store, but said that he would try to stop by the creek on his way back from Greenwood. As Easy strolled to Worley's creek, the countryside stretched before him like a great quilt of multi-colored squares. Rambling though pastures, over ditches and rough terrain Easy would occasionally shift the watermelon from arm to arm. The countryside was a safe place to play, explore and since childhood had created many new adventures. He picked up his pace and hurried along the way because Worley's creek had beckoned.

Tulsa's Black Wall Street
A story of Greenwood Oklahoma

He finally reached the path that was tucked away at the back of a cow pasture leading into the woods. The path swerved back and forth unpredictably like the steps of a staggering drunk. Except for some intertwined tree roots, the path was fairly clear. Curls of vibrant green ivy also lined the narrow path and various large trees arched over the path. This narrow understated path was the only way into the children's watery oasis. Upon reaching his destination, Easy scanned the area around the creek and found himself there all alone. Not a person was seen or sound could be heard either close at hand or in the far off distance. Easy sat on the edge of the creek's grassy bank and placed his watermelon in a shallow part of water to cool. Silence hung in the air thick and heavy like a blanket as he unwound from the day. As he stood and once again scanned the area to look around him, Easy was somehow comforted by the quiet. The air was sweet and there was a light breeze; it was a perfect day for a swim. Suddenly his lips bore the semblance of a smile as he had a thought. Being alone, Easy decided to take advantage of his own paradise to skinny dip.

Looking around one final time, Easy quickly slipped out of his clothes and dashed into the water. He loved the feel of the water on his naked body.

Tulsa's Black Wall Street

A story of Greenwood Oklahoma

He swam out to where the water was deepest then lay back in the water, letting his limbs do the thinking for him. He found the water refreshing. Now oblivious to his surroundings Easy let the water take all of his worries away. He stretched out his arms, opened his palms and released all his bodily tensions. Suddenly, Easy thought that he had heard a noise coming from the direction of the woods. Dropping his body below the water's surface, he scanned the banks, but saw nothing. He shouted out, "CT is that you?" However, there was no response; nothing but silence. His heart began to thump hard in his chest as he once again shouted, "Stop playing CT; if you are up there say something." Once again, there was still no response, only silence. Certain he had heard a noise and growing increasingly anxious Easy said to himself, "Damn!!! This is just what I need, to be naked in the water and have some redneck cracker sneak up on me." Rolling his eyes, he cautiously swam to shallower water so his feet could touch the bottom. He then carefully walked back to the bank and retrieved his clothing. Cautiously he put on his clothes while simultaneously looking around and listening intently.

Tulsa's Black Wall Street

A story of Greenwood Oklahoma

All of a sudden he heard the noises once again…footsteps. As a young child, Easy was taught the methods of distinguishing noises and footsteps by his grandfather. He knew straightaway the approaching footsteps were from someone who had not learned to walk quietly. Each footfall was chaotically spaced from the last, with no rhythm at all. Whoever it was lacked confidence and was likely scared. Keeping his eyes glued to the trees, Easy determined the person trudging was likely of no immediate threat, but he still remained cautious.

Suddenly, after seeing a slightly silhouetted figure through the trees, he heard a melodic "Hi Easy". Despite a struggle, Easy tried but was unable to hide the shock that registered on his face. "Emma, you almost scared the hell out of me. What are you doing out here alone" Easy asked? Smiling Emma said, "Ma sent me and Joseph to take a letter and some vegetables to Preacher Boyd. She also wanted us to dig-up and bring her back some sassafras roots. To save time Joseph asked me to dig up the sassafras roots and he would deliver the stuff to Pastor Boyd. He is going to stop back by here on his way back. I thought I heard someone at the creek so I wanted to see who it was." Nodding his head, Easy said, "I know how your Ma is, so I will give you a hand and save you guys some time."

Tulsa's Black Wall Street
A story of Greenwood Oklahoma

Continuing he said, "I have a watermelon cooling in the creek; you and Joseph can help me eat it. I was expecting CT, but I believe he is going to be a no show." As Easy began brushing debris off his clothing he told Emma that he had just taken a quick dip.

What Easy did not know was Emma had watched him the entire time of his skinny dip. Her eyes was locked on him as she collected every inch; every muscle of his beautiful brown body. She had never seen a boy naked before. For that matter, except for church meetings, she had not seen a lot of boy's period. Putting it mildly, Emma was more than intrigued by what she saw. Emma was 15 and under the surface she was battling feelings that she had never experienced before. Looking at Easy now and thinking of his impressive brown physique made her skin tingle. Emma's cheeks flushed hot. There were also butterflies… no eagles… in her stomach, but strangely it felt good. She bit her lip, desperately trying to determine how to start a conversation or if she should start a conversation, telling Easy what she had seen. Emma's heart pounded and her knees began knocking as she began to realize that Easy had aroused her sexual interest.

Tulsa's Black Wall Street

A story of Greenwood Oklahoma

As Emma's heart pounded in her throat, threatening to break out, she couldn't find her voice. Then in that instant he turned and caught her eye; before she could turn away with shyness a smile spread across her face. Emma was one of his friends that Easy could always read relatively easily. It was clear of Emma's interest in him by her movements, actions and the look in her eyes. Easy had never much noticed Emma before, especially in that way. She was his friend's sister, the trio had been friends since they were kids and besides she was white.

As her eyes wandered around trying to avoid contact, Easy's eyes stayed locked on Emma. She wasn't a little girl anymore. Easy suddenly felt his mouth go dry. This wasn't like when they were kids. Emma finally looked his way, making eye contact, her mouth forming a smile, "Hey, Easy... I couldn't find my voice to tell you, but I did see you swimming earlier. I had never seen a boy naked before, but I must admit that I liked what I saw." With her heart somersaulting, Emma stepped closer to Easy trying to decide what would happen next. Confused and with mixed feelings she was sexually curious but weary of her reputation. The thrill of taking a chance was more than she could resist and from her heart she asked Easy, "Would you like to kiss me?"

Tulsa's Black Wall Street

A story of Greenwood Oklahoma

For the first time ever Easy felt like if he opened his mouth nothing witty or interesting would come out. Rather than respond Easy stepped closer and hugged her. During the embrace, he brushed his lips on hers. His hand traveled the distance from her shoulders to her buttocks and touched them. After kissing her, a small but teasing smile crept upon her face. Goosebumps lined her skin, not the kind than one gets in the cold, but the kind one gets when nothing else matters except right here, right now. As they began a second kiss, the moment was shattered by a scream. "EMMA…EMMA…Where are you," Joseph shouted? She pulled away from Easy, gathered herself before shouting back in response, "We are over here."

When Joseph finally made his way to them, the trio gathered sassafras roots and ate watermelon before going their separate ways.

Tulsa's Black Wall Street

A story of Greenwood Oklahoma

Chapter 4

When you think…Wealth… Abundance… Affluence… Prosperity… Success… or whatever you decided to call it…that in a nutshell described Greenwood!!!!

For as long as blacks could recall, they were viewed by whites as merely subhuman; more like beasts than men. White people believed that a race's superiority or inferiority, social and moral traits were predetermined by his or her race. Accepting this as fact, based solely on color, whites justified the enslavement and mistreatment of black people. Black people were targeted, enslaved and discriminated against based solely on race. Once institutionalized, these racist beliefs became a behavioral norm that supported this racist line of thinking. White people's unquestionable belief that blacks were subservient and inferior creatures influenced their support of slavery, legal codes and eventually war. The South's loss of the civil war guaranteed more hatred and enmity for blacks. This hatred toward blacks was passed like a dark flame from one generation to the next resulting in institutional inequities.

Tulsa's Black Wall Street
A story of Greenwood Oklahoma

These inequities were manifested in the distribution of wealth, power, and opportunities afforded to the black race. However now, a merely 45 years post-civil war, Greenwood happens. The widely held racist image that was promulgated about black people as ignorant, lazy, unsophisticated sub-humans was about to be proven as very wrong and untruthful. Whites became concerned that blacks would prove by their deeds that they were not inadequate. One of their deepest fears of the Ku Klux Klan was that the evidence of Greenwood would demonstrate that blacks were not inferior as had been previously portrayed. In fact, it could now be reasonably argued that they were, in fact, on equal footing with whites. This reality did not sit well with racist whites and they refused to accept it.

During slavery, not all black people accepted their perceived inadequacy. Blacks, in general, were strong of faith and had an unshakable belief in God and themselves. Despite the brutality of slavery, institutionalized oppression and persistent disenfranchisement measures black people proved to be remarkably resilient. Now, a mere 45 years past slavery, blacks were comprehensively refuting white stereotypes. They believed themselves to be the children of God and there was nothing that Tulsa could do to stop or obstruct their blessings.

Tulsa's Black Wall Street

A story of Greenwood Oklahoma

Blacks thought of Greenwood as their City upon a Hill. Biblically, they were referencing "A City upon a Hill" which is a phrase from the parable of Salt and Light in Jesus's Sermon on the Mount. In Matthew 5:14, he tells his listeners, "You are the light of the world. A city that is set on a hill cannot be hidden."

The measures enacted by Tulsa in an effort to disenfranchise blacks proved unsuccessful. Whites became frustrated over the success of Greenwood and of their business acumen. The ability of blacks and their ability to create a self-sustaining exclusive black enclave was a completely unintended consequence. Instead of respect for what blacks had accomplished in Greenwood, whites grew angry. Hatred crawled under the skin of white people and pumped fear into their veins. The Ku Klux Klan exploded with anger. They howled that the success of blacks was a personal affront against whites and could "very well alter the natural order of things." The Klan wanted to reverse the progress and predictably they were not above using violence to achieve their objective. The Klan was not about to humble themselves to "those apes."

Tulsa's Black Wall Street
A story of Greenwood Oklahoma

Reminiscent of the dramatic duel with Moses, when Pharaoh hardened his heart rather than humble himself to God, under the Klan's influence Tulsa's leaders hardened their hearts. With dogged determination Tulsa tightened their segregated laws with the intent to escalate racial oppression. About the same time, President Woodrow Wilson introduced segregation into federal government agencies. Black employees were separated from other workers in offices, restrooms, and cafeterias. Some were downgraded; others discharged on fictitious grounds. By the year 1914 Tulsa was so racist and segregated that it was the only city in America that boasted of segregated telephone booths.

As segregation tightened and racial oppression escalated the black leaders in Greenwood rejected a conciliatory approach. They were fully ready to forcefully defend the promise of equality under the law. As Hezekiah so eloquently expressed it, "There is nothing civilized about colored people cowering so that white people can feel good about themselves. All people are meant to excel; not just some of us. Allowing white people to bully us or crush our dreams would not serve our children well." Tulsa's efforts to silence blacks politically, helped to foster an atmosphere for violence.

Tulsa's Black Wall Street

A story of Greenwood Oklahoma

Although overtly condemning such activity, covertly they encouraged random lawlessness and lynching or provided a defense for anti-black actions. A rising tide of passion grew within the Greenwood community. Greenwood's black print media pulled no punches in their fiery protest approach. Their editorials suggested readers arm themselves if armed lynchers come into Greenwood. They further proposed meeting white mobs and retaliating with sticks and clubs and guns.

Over the next couple years fear and propaganda between the two communities created a politically tense environment. However that uneasy alliance between Tulsa and Greenwood was put to a test one perfect autumn Saturday in 1917. The weather was gorgeous. It was the kind of weather that felt like a kiss of summer without the fiery heat of August. The blue skies, no wind and ambient temperature; it was more like an absence of weather really. Early Saturday morning, a black man name Walter Oakley walked into Tulsa heading to the town's livery-stable. He had heard that the owner was looking to hire a livery-stable keeper. Walter was accompanied in Tulsa by his cousin Arthur Oakley. Black's rightfully believed unless you were employed in Tulsa it was best not to be alone.

Tulsa's Black Wall Street
A story of Greenwood Oklahoma

They believed there to be a degree of safety in numbers, so to speak. There were occasions when black domestics and hired help were subjected to harassment and violence when traveling alone. The Klan had made its hostile intentions clear about retribution and the black community listened. When Walter approached the livery-stable a dog charged from inside the building and attacked him. After being bitten on his leg by the dog, Walter kicked the dog away in self-defense. The dog gave out a loud yelp and ran away. Walter glanced over and saw Mr. Wilson staring. Walter could see Mr. Wilson's face was smoldering underneath his stony expression. His face turned the color of an over-ripe tomato as suppressed anger and hatred showed in his eyes. Confused, Walter reasonably thought Mr. Wilson most certainly could not be upset at him for kicking the dog.

After all he had been bitten by the dog and was merely protecting himself. With his fists clenched, eyes squinting meanly, Mr. Wilson walked up to Walter. Snarling more than he spoke, Mr. Wilson asked "Nigger, didn't you see that sign telling you to beware of the dog?" "No Sir Boss man", Walter responded respectfully. Explaining he continued, "I can't read Mr. Wilson Sir."

Tulsa's Black Wall Street

A story of Greenwood Oklahoma

Exasperated Mr. Wilson asked, "why did you kick my dog, clearly he was just being friendly?" Once again in a polite and respectful manner Walter said, "No sir, the dog bit me Boss." Walter's response did not sit well with Mr. Wilson and he shot back nastily, "I say the dog was playing with you and you say he wasn't. Are you calling me a liar boy?" After Mr. Wilson's retort, every eye inside the stable immediately turned in Walter's direction. A group of white men began walking toward him. Right off Walter knew that he had hit the wrong button which was an unfortunate set of circumstances. From experience he also knew the situation was bad and would only get worse.

Fortunately for Walter, Tulsa's Sheriff just happened to be in the vicinity. Like a lot of local residents, Sheriff Eugene Champ was lured to Tulsa by the land rush. Formerly a Deputy Sheriff in Kansas, he was appointed Sheriff by Tulsa's Mayor because of his law enforcement experience. Kansans strongly favored the cause of the Union. His family fought for the North during the Civil War and as a man of character, Sheriff Champ was anti-slavery. Despite his anti-slavery views, being principled, he may not have liked them, but he enforced Tulsa's segregationist laws.

Tulsa's Black Wall Street
A story of Greenwood Oklahoma

He tried to be just and do the right thing in all circumstances but, he was no saint or hero. However he was civil, honest, fair and always candid. He was respected by the black citizens in Greenwood for his courteousness and candor. As the situation evolved a crowd quickly began to assemble. In a raised voice Mr. Wilson was now demanding that Walter be jailed. He accused Walter of vagrancy, disrespecting a white person and injuring his dog. The gathered crowd began rumblings and echoing Mr. Wilson's words, demanding Walter pay for the crimes. From behind Sheriff Champ, someone in the crowd yelled. "That was a damn good dog and he is a heap more valuable than that nigger." Recognizing the precariousness of the situation, Sheriff Champ decided to arrest Walter. The charges were dubious, but Walter was being jailed for his own safety.

Before being led away, Walter asked Arthur to tell his older brother Bill in Greenwood what happened. Arthur rushed back to Greenwood to find Bill. As he hurried back, his brain kept screaming, "Go back. Do not leave Walter alone in that town." However, as Walter requested Arthur continued going forward to Greenwood. As his panic grew, Arthur's adrenaline levels rose, he quickened his pace into a full out run.

Tulsa's Black Wall Street

A story of Greenwood Oklahoma

The air was unexpectedly warm for autumn as sweat covered his body and his heart beat harder and faster. Arthur normally did not move this fast unless there was something after him but now there was no other option. After frantically asking around, Arthur located Bill's whereabouts. It was late afternoon when Arthur finally found Bill at Willie Brown's Barrelhouse (also called a Juke Joint by some).

Being a perfect autumn day, Bill was enjoying the surprisingly pleasant weather. Bill and a group of friends had gathered at Willie Brown's place to welcome Percy Cook back home from the Army. Greenwood was Percy's home and he was returning from his basic training at Camp Logan in Houston, Texas. The black press sided with France against blacks serving in the military, because of its purported commitment to racial equality. In agreement, Percy deemed the government's cry of Americanism as hypocritical. Percy felt he owed "American democracy" no sense of loyalty considering the daily inequalities blacks faced. However, the United States government mobilized the entire nation for war, and blacks were expected to do their part. The military instituted a draft in order to create an army capable of winning the war.

Tulsa's Black Wall Street

A story of Greenwood Oklahoma

Percy was drafted into the United States Army and was on military leave visiting home before heading to Europe. Looking sharp and confident in his military uniform, Percy was mesmerizing while describing the many sights he had seen. He also told of all the different "brothers" he had the opportunity to meet from all the different parts of the country. Percy boasted of being able to see a totally different country; especially France. The French nation was fascinated with black culture. Black soldiers arriving in France received a warm welcome from French civilians, who exhibited little overt racism. One of Percy's Army buddies from North Carolina recalled to him, "They treated us with respect, not at all like back home."

As Percy weaved an account of his experiences, Easy's eyes were locked on his every move and gesture. Easy was captivated by the vivid pictorial account and offered his undivided attention. This was his life. Percy was talking real life events and real people. Alcohol was an integral component before, during and following Percy's bragging. Everyone laughed while joking, selling "wolf tickets", "signifying" and "playing the dozens". They also picked individual teams for a competitive game horse shoes.

Tulsa's Black Wall Street
A story of Greenwood Oklahoma

Between pitching horse shoes and bouncing momma jokes like a kid's rubber ball back and forth among themselves, it was a fun time. Truthfully there was likely an uncertainty whether they really got wittier as the evening wore on or if it was just the effect of the moonshine making everything seem so much funnier. However, little did anyone know at the time, that the fun and merriment was about to end abruptly.

Tulsa's Black Wall Street
A story of Greenwood Oklahoma

Chapter 5

Arthur ran up to Bill, who was shooting dice at the time, covered in sweat and tired as hell. Bill was on a roll and became angry as Arthur interrupted his game. Surrounded by his friends anxious to get back to gambling Bill asked, "What the hell are you doing? Can't you see you are interrupting the game?" The exertion brought on breathlessness like the air around him was devoid of oxygen. His ribs heaved up and down but there seemed to be of no benefit, so he slumped to the ground. He was weary from the run and the burden of what had happened to Walter. Finally, after drawing controlled gasps, was he able to reveal what happened to Walter.

Arthur's news dampened everyone's mood and immediately ended the dice game and Percy's welcome home celebration. Just moments earlier the men had been laughing, joking, pitching horseshoes and shooting dice, but now they all stood silent. The news of Walter's fate caused an icy chill to run down Bill's spine.

Tulsa's Black Wall Street

A story of Greenwood Oklahoma

Next there was a flash of anger with Bill saying, "Black people have been abused for years while praying for and patiently waiting for some kind of change in heart from white people. I don't think it will ever happen and we are fooling ourselves if we think it will. I'm done with this the meek are going to be inheriting the earth bullshit. I am a man and starting right now I am going to act like one. I may go down, but I will preserve my dignity and go down fighting." Bill's imagination went into overdrive. His panic grew stronger by the minute as his mental faculties gave way to emotions. From exasperation he began cursing and moving around erratically. Understanding his anger, a rage quickly spread through the crowd. Easy watched Bill closely and could see the silent panic on his face. He could almost feel Bill's fury, building like an unstoppable snowball in the pit of his stomach. Easy knew that alcohol and extreme anger was a volatile mix fraught with danger. He trusted his father to know what to do, so he rushed home.

After explaining the situation about Walter to Hezekiah, Easy asked his father to intercede on Bill's behalf. After consulting with O.W. Gurley and Reverend Stubbs, the three men decided to visit Sheriff Champ in Tulsa, with Easy in tow.

Tulsa's Black Wall Street
A story of Greenwood Oklahoma

It was early evening when they arrived, found the jailhouse in disarray. Sheriff Champ was disheveled and bleeding from a head wound. The sheriff explained that he heard the buzz of an angry crowd heading toward the direction of the jail. He secured the jail cell and headed outside to intercede on Walter's behalf. Having barely stepped outside, someone cold cocked him and knocked him unconscious. After aiding the Sheriff in regaining his composure, he offered his assistance. The Sheriff said, "I could use your help, If you would consider assisting me." I am going to try and find Walter. I hope you all know that I don't share the views of the people who have done this. I can only promise that if they harm you, they will have to harm me too." He handed each man a shotgun before starting out on their search.

At approximately 8 pm, the men found Walter Oakley hanging from a big cottonwood tree at the Wagon Bridge northwest of the city. The body was still hanging there with hands behind his back and flies buzzing around him. Walter's body had been soaked in coal oil and set afire. The corpse was almost devoid of skin. Without eyelids the milky eyes stared into the distant sky while his lip-less mouth hung open.... And the smell!!

Tulsa's Black Wall Street

A story of Greenwood Oklahoma

The odor was the most disturbing thing that Easy had ever smelled. Borrowing Easy's knife, the sheriff cut Walter down and asked the Reverend to say a few words over him. The stench of burning flesh caused Easy to heave. The nausea clawed at his throat, and he tried to force down the bile, but it was too late. He lurched forward and sunk to his knees. Chunks of partially digested chicken spewed out of his coughing, choking mouth. His stomach kept on contracting violently and forcing everything up and out. As he turned to rise from his knees, he thought he saw someone in the brush. He said nothing at the moment, but desperately hoped that he was wrong about what he thought he had seen. A short distance after leaving Easy lied and told the other men he had dropped his knife at the site. He informed them of his intent to retrieve the knife and catch up with them. Sheriff Champ suggested that he hold on to the shotgun. Through the woods, Easy quietly approached the Wagon Bridge from the back side. He stopped by an old oak tree, listened intently and carefully surveyed the area. Suddenly he spotted what he was looking for; someone crouching in the bushes.

Easy pulled out his knife and turned it over in his hands, feeling the weight of it.

Tulsa's Black Wall Street
A story of Greenwood Oklahoma

His father helped him make the knife and it was designed to fit exactly into the palm of Easy's hand. It was no heavier than a domestic kitchen blade but durable and extremely sharp. The knife was sharp enough to cut on first contact with minimum pressure. Easy's grandfather was old school and believed in knives. The old man once told Easy that guns were noisy and could jam, but the knife was a true friend. It will do its job instantly and it will never let you down. Easy's face shifted from neutral to a frown as he stealthily began to move toward the man from behind. After reaching his target, Easy placed his knife to the man's throat. Using minimum pressure, a small amount of blood began to trickle from the man's neck. Cold and ruthlessly Easy said, "Jr. give me just one good reason why I should not cut your damned head off." Kenneth Jr.'s was the face Easy recognized earlier hiding in the bushes.

Easy was not a complex person. He was very charismatic with an easy demeanor however much like his father he grappled internally with the biblical concept of turning the other cheek. He was compassionate with those he cared for; he was gracious and respectful to those he met; he was not easily provoked; very slow to anger.

Tulsa's Black Wall Street
A story of Greenwood Oklahoma

However once he became angry, it was advisable to either steer clear or run for cover. It was also general knowledge around Greenwood that Easy knew his way around and was quite handy with a knife. He did not consider himself a "tough guy" and felt no need to ever prove himself; and very few people tried him. Jr. knew that Easy was not a person to be trifled with. If Easy threatened to cut his head off, Jr. knew the precariousness of his situation. As much as he tried to hold it in, the pain came out like an uproar from deep within. Now sobbing with tears streaming from his blue eyes, Jr. begged Easy for his life saying he had nothing to do with the lynching. He was left behind by his father as a punishment for not wanting to either inflict damage on Walter's body or take a souvenir. When he turned his face to Easy, Jr. was a picture of grief, loss and devastation. It was the face of one who had suffered before and didn't know if he could do it again. Suddenly noticing Jr.'s shirt was soiled with bile and smelling the pungent stench of vomit, Easy eased up.

Easy had known Jr. since childhood and believed him to be telling the truth. "Speak quickly and tell me the whole story or I promise that I will gut you like a fish" Easy demanded.

Tulsa's Black Wall Street
A story of Greenwood Oklahoma

Tears burst forth from Jr., like water from a bursting dam, spilling down his face. As he cried there was rawness, as if the pain was still an open wound. He clasped onto Easy's leg for support, and his whole body trembled. Kneeling there, dominated by a profound sadness and with fatigue engraved on his face Jr. told Easy the whole story.

Kenneth Sr. had gathered a bunch of his cronies espousing white privilege and condemning the actions of the "nigger vagrant." He complained that niggers over in Greenwood were doing just as good if not better than white folks and that was not natural. He complained about how lowly vagrant niggers were coming into their town and talking any kind of way. They could not allow white people to be talked to like that. Although it was not true, he told how the nigger stabbed and killed a white man's dog. He insisted that they could not have their property disrespected. A burning rage hissed through the crowd like deathly poison. It was a fear that brought rage; a hot burning anger that sought violence. The wrath of their fear engulfed all morality and demanded harm. Kenneth Sr. demanded that the nigger pay for his crimes in their city. Kenneth Sr. stationed himself behind the jail and signaled the crowd. As the mob approached the jail, they all concealed their faces.

Tulsa's Black Wall Street
A story of Greenwood Oklahoma

When Sheriff Champ stepped out to address the crowd, Kenneth Sr. struck the Sheriff from behind with a stick of wood. After dragging Walter from the jail they began beating him with clubs, shovels and bricks. They stripped him naked, soaked him in coal oil and threw him into the wagon while taunting him all along. When they arrived at the wagon bridge Walter was thrown off the wagon where they encircled him continuing the punching, beating and kicking. A noose was placed around his neck and he was again soaked in coal oil. People in the mob cut off different parts of his body as a souvenir before they hung him from the cottonwood tree. After hanging Walter, Kenneth Sr. smiled broadly and sinisterly said to the mob, "okay boys time for a coon cooking." He then set Walter on fire. Helplessly poor Walter prayed and shrieked in agony as the flames burned his flesh. However, in a macabre manner his cries of pain were drowned out by yells and jeers from the mob.

Walter's cries began to grow fainter and it became evident that he was losing consciousness. The armed mob aimed their weapons and used Walter's body for target practice. Almost every member of the mob fired a volley of shots into Walter's swinging charred corpse.

Tulsa's Black Wall Street
A story of Greenwood Oklahoma

Jr. did not have the stomach to cut off a souvenir from Walter's body and did not participate. Despite his father's demands, Jr. also refused to set Walter on fire. When Kenneth Sr. started the fire, Jr.'s head began to spin, he became nauseated and vomited.

Kenneth Sr. and about five of his friends encircled Jr. teasing and calling him names. The old man had nothing short of disgust on his face, almost hatred toward his son, as his face reddened with anger. Kenneth Sr. began poking his finger in Jr.'s chest and taunted him by repeatedly saying, "I will not have a weakling for a son and you will not shame me." He continued to say, "I would rather have you swinging up there beside that nigger than embarrass me. The fine men assembled here are patriots. We all share an alliance of the same values. We also have a strong pride, love and devotion to the white race. A patriot must always be ready and willing to defend the white race. You are not fit to walk with us. " Kenneth Sr. told Jr. that he needed an attitude adjustment. To make his point, the old man demanded that Jr. remain at the hanging site to reflect on who he was. His father's reaction in front of everyone caused Jr. great embarrassment, so he remained there too shocked to move.

Tulsa's Black Wall Street

A story of Greenwood Oklahoma

As members of the mob departed for their homes, Kenneth Sr. could be overheard laughing and asking jocularly, "Wasn't that some barbecue we had boys?"

In describing the mutilation and then setting a man on fire Jr. told Easy, "I was mortified, frozen to the spot. I felt traumatized. It was right in front of me but I somehow did not want to believe it had really happened. I just stood there looking around and soaking in the cruel laughter. Easy, that stench will live with me forever. I will never forget this day as long as I live." With his shoulders slumped and eyes cast down in a mournful gaze Jr. continued, "The way he treated me, I just want the earth to open up and swallow me whole. After all, I am his son. We had a loving relationship or so I thought until that moment." He paused momentarily and then said, "Easy, I am afraid to die. Can you find it in your heart to forgive me? Are you going to kill me?"

Looking at Jr. with a mixture of pity and disgust, Easy responded, "No I am not going to kill you. I believe your story and that you are genuinely remorseful. I think you now realize that racism is sinful. All blood flow red and every person whether black or white is your brother.

Tulsa's Black Wall Street
A story of Greenwood Oklahoma

You have been a good friend and you have a conscious, so there is hope for you. I hope God shows you mercy. But I hope your crazy cracker ass father burn in hell."

As it starting to get darker Easy helped Jr. to his feet and told him to "Forgive yourself for your faults and your mistakes and move on. Hell was not for ordinary people who tried their best and failed because all people fail. To be imperfect is just part of being human and God's love is for us all. Despite your father's teachings, make the effort give colored people the courtesy of your compassion and respect. Now get out of my sight." Jr. told Easy, "This is the second time that my life has been in your hands. You saved me from downing once when we were kids and you did not turn me into the Sheriff this time." With a chuckle Jr. continued, "It is funny how a face my father has been trying to teach me to despise, hate, and fear has me comfort. I have no need to fear you Easy, I fear not knowing the truth. I owe you and I promise on my life that I will never forget all that you have done. Trust me." With that they both went their separate ways.

Part of Jr. felt almost cheated. He deserved and wanted punishment, but what he got was forgiveness.

Tulsa's Black Wall Street
A story of Greenwood Oklahoma

He thought, maybe God is Love after all. Reliving Easy's words, Jr. did not want to run or hide from what he had done; he wanted to own up to it. If he could relive the day, he would go to that jail and release Walter before the mob arrived. He would tell Walter to go home where he'd be safe from white people. Jr. prayed on his way home. He begged God for deliverance from this sin and its consequences. He prayed for salvation.

Tulsa's Black Wall Street
A story of Greenwood Oklahoma

Chapter 6

His heart pounded as one question continued to race through his mind, As Easy rode to catch up with the other men; what kind of men are these and what could be the root for such hate of another human being? Twenty four hours earlier Walter was alive and breathing. His entire life was in front of him. Walter was a good guy and he didn't deserve what came to him. Easy couldn't think how anyone could earn an ending like that. Suddenly an event, Easy thought long buried came to his mind that frightened him. He thought what if someone other than her brother Joseph had showed up on the day that he kissed Emma? What if Kenneth Sr. or one of his friends had come along? That could very well have been Easy's fate after kissing a white girl; tortured and hung. As hard as he tried he could not dislodge this terrible thought from his mind. The thought of how he could have been a victim of racist brutality scared him. His thoughts not only scared him but they also angered him. It angered him so that he wanted to kill every member of the mob who murdered Walter.

Tulsa's Black Wall Street
A story of Greenwood Oklahoma

Easy imagined mob members being thrown down a well and the Greenwood community was tossing in shovels of dirt. He imagined the crowd cheering as the mob began to cry and beg for mercy while they were choking to death with a mouth full of muck. Reflecting back Easy was happy that after the kiss, he pursued the relationship no further. Even on that warm autumn evening, thinking of the blood thirsty white men who murdered blacks indiscriminately made Easy shiver.

On the following morning Greenwood was abuzz about Walter's lynching. Rumors were flying thick and spread quickly throughout the community. O.W., Hezekiah and Easy did not disclose the gruesomeness of the death however, that fact did not deter the rumor mill. Bill and his friends were out for blood. The young people began gathering knives, guns, axes, farm implements and making homemade explosives. Religious leaders request's for prayer and calm was falling on deaf ears. One young man responded, "By all means pray, but white people must earn our prayers. Do white people pray before they brutalize and hang our Negro brothers? Do white people pray as they rape our Negro sisters?

Tulsa's Black Wall Street

A story of Greenwood Oklahoma

Do white people pray as Negro children pay the price for their evil deeds? I believe in Heaven and I believe in prayer, but I am tired of praying as I carry flowers to Negro funerals. I think we will find weapons are more effective in addition to prayer at this point in time. I will pray that while I am shooting them, my weapon does not misfire."

This younger group of people had heard of slavery's brutality through their elders and finally they had seen enough. They did not see their expectations as unreasonable. This group of young people wanted nothing more than the same chance in life as their white counterpart. They wanted a job, security, the same chance for happiness and a family that white people took for granted. They wanted fair law and order. They wanted democracy. The newer generation of blacks saw these as their birthright. The militancy by younger blacks in Greenwood was ticking like the timer on a bomb. The church could not stop it, reverse it, or slow it down. Each tick dragged Greenwood forward, closer to a possible violent confrontation. Nervousness over the potential severity resulted in Reverend Stubbs calling a meeting between other church leaders and prominent black businessmen. The situation was regarded as serious by those assembled and needed to be dealt with.

Tulsa's Black Wall Street

A story of Greenwood Oklahoma

The group agreed that Reverend Stubbs, O.W. and Hezekiah would act as a delegation from Greenwood. The three men had acknowledged their previous meeting and going with Sheriff Champ to recover Walter's body. There were lots of people who talk the talk, but these men had a history of walking the walk. Because of the restlessness in Greenwood's young blacks, this delegation did not want to delay a meeting with Sheriff Champ. They left immediately for the meeting, but Hezekiah requested they stop to pick up Easy. Hezekiah told the other men that Easy had met with Jr. and knew identities of some mob members. He felt this information could be of some benefit.

The mood of the meeting was oppressively solemn. Hezekiah was very blunt with the Sheriff and spoke with a coldness Easy had never heard before, especially to a white. Hezekiah told the Sheriff that black people in Greenwood were angry about what happened to Walter. He said younger blacks feel like they were drowning in helplessness with little hope of being saved. They were growing extremely impatient over mistreatment and tempers were boiling. He reminded the Sheriff of how by Tulsa's very laws they had deliberately placed a target on dark skin. Rather than inspire dreams, the city was instilling mistrust.

Tulsa's Black Wall Street
A story of Greenwood Oklahoma

Hezekiah promised, "If nothing is done soon, the city's inaction to create a sense of community will lead to blood on the streets; both your streets and our streets." Silence in the room fell with the speed of a bullet. Sheriff Champ's heart twisted and sunk with nerves as the men sat in front of him staring intently. He refused to look away, even as his lips trembled and his shoulders heaved with emotion.

Slowly, his panic flowed away as he told the group that he was willing to listen and work with them in any way to prevent trouble. Shuffling through some papers on top of his desk, he picked up a small folder. Holding the folder and with his voice quivering he said, "Sometimes we see something that frightens us. I asked the city to perform an autopsy on Walter and provide me an official cause of death for investigative purposes. I want to be open and honest so I want you to see the results. I must admit that the savagery of these results sickened me. The medical examiner's report recorded the official cause of death as multiple gunshot wounds by miscreants unknown. The report also noted other wounds suffered were missing fingers, missing ears, missing penis and tentacles." Handing the folder to Reverend Stubbs, the Sheriff paused briefly to regain his composure.

Tulsa's Black Wall Street

A story of Greenwood Oklahoma

"Gentlemen I am as disgusted about this report and what had happened as I know you are" the Sheriff assured the group.

He continued by saying, "These mobs use lynching as a means to terrorize and exert social control over colored people. Taking a trophy is a part of their sick ritual. Mutilating bodies is a sick way, in their warped mind, to demonstrate white male supremacy and black male impotence. I beg you to not let the results of this autopsy leave this room. To avoid a race war, people can't know about what happened at Wagon Bridge. I can't command the city, hell I struggle to even command my pet dog. However, gentlemen I refuse to be powerless or not even try to put the power of this office into action. I want you to know that my heart is in the right place. Hope is a bright star in a hopelessly dark universe, but I want to offer your young people hope. I am open to your input."

Turning his attention to Easy, Sheriff Champ said, "You are a part of the new generation. Tell me Easy, what are your thoughts?" Easy quickly looked in the direction of his father, as if seeking approval to respond. Understanding his son's uncertainty, Hezekiah offered him a nod of approval and said "go ahead".

Tulsa's Black Wall Street

A story of Greenwood Oklahoma

With butterflies in his stomach and his head buzzing Easy searched for the right words to say. Fortunately for Easy, the nervousness that travelled throughout his body never made it to his facial muscles or skin. He could almost feel all the eyes on him and silence in the air as Sheriff Champ awaited his feedback. After another quick glance in Hezekiah's direction, Easy let out an understated sigh and began to speak. "My friends are talking about the bad things that are coming. They have a mistrust of generations. They don't trust white people for the hateful things they have done. But they also don't trust older colored people for not fighting back. They see the whole generation as lost and wish they would get out of their way. Without something drastic, I don't see any way of avoiding violence. They feel like the sheep being willingly herded for slaughter, only the sheep don't know where it's going; but they do. Trust me when I tell you that they may be going to slaughter, but unlike the sheep, my friends think they are invincible and will not be going to slaughter so easily." Then Easy stopped, glanced sideways at his father and turned back to the Sheriff. A bit uncertain, but not so much that he cared, Easy wanted to offer an "oh, by the way."

Tulsa's Black Wall Street

A story of Greenwood Oklahoma

He told Sheriff Champ "For what it's worth you have a lot of hatemongers and I know who they are. Some are obvious and some not so obvious. They are the kind that will throw a rock then hide their hand. But the ring leader is Big Kenneth Chase. He is that one withered tree in Tulsa's woods. His blaze can cause the whole forest to burn."

After Easy spoke Hezekiah was beaming with pride. One could almost hear the strain of the buttons to stay on his shirt as he pumped out his chest. Looking at his son, he smiled and said "Until you have a son of your own, you will never know the joy, the love beyond feeling that is in my heart." Recognizing this as an ideal time, Easy told his father that there was something they needed to discuss afterward. A bit puzzled but still filled with pride Hezekiah simply responded, "Okay son. We will talk later."

Hezekiah turned his attention to other members of the delegation and asked, "I think that my son has summed up the young people situation pretty well; wouldn't you all agree?" With everyone now nodding their head in agreement, he told Sheriff Champ, "If we are going to be serious about addressing this situation, there is no way Tulsa can continue to stay rooted in the past rage.

Tulsa's Black Wall Street
A story of Greenwood Oklahoma

That rage destroys from the inside, corrupts a sense of community into one of division, hate and distrust. The mistrust won't be hard to fix so you must be willing to push ahead and challenge city officials. Everyone should be clear in understanding that the alternative will be very unpleasant. We could engage in an armed struggle, but what is the point? Lives would be taken, the divide would widen and the possibility of restoring friendly relations would be broken beyond repair. We would be two people stranded on a shared island of fear and uncertainty, without any rafts of hope. I propose we end this potential for violence; end it for all of our futures. I ask you…no I beg you and all whites to search deep within your hearts, for understanding." Deep in his heart Hezekiah knew there were times when a retreat from conflict was bravery, not cowardice. That sometimes it took fortitude to temporarily backtrack from a fight and find another route around to eventual victory. For a few young men to rashly attack whites without a coherent plan, just to satisfy a blood-lust, would be foolish. It would lead to the pointless deaths of many innocents; to include women and children. Realistically, Greenwood was outmanned and outgunned.

After considerable discussion, the group arrived on a plan that was agreeable.

Tulsa's Black Wall Street

A story of Greenwood Oklahoma

They developed a strategic plan with the intended actions to develop mutual trust within. As part of the plan, a black counsel would be established to meet with the Sheriff monthly. Sheriff Champ agreed to add two black deputies to the Tulsa police department. There would be input from the established black counsel in the selection and hiring of the new black police officers. Greenwood would provide the resources to pay the salary for one of the new officers. They would also fund the construction a jail in Greenwood. In theory, keeping black arrestees jailed in Greenwood would provide greater safety and security to minorities while in custody.

On their way home Easy told his father, "Dad I have been thinking and there is something I'd like to discuss with you. You taught me that growing up is all about responsibilities. You have given me the wisdom to know when to follow, the courage when I must lead, and the heart to stay true when the waters get rough. You always told me that life is about making decisions and accepting responsibility for those decisions. You've also told me, even if it was a poor decision; that it may be an ugly baby but it was my baby and I had to rock it. I never realized that growing was so confusing and so hard.

Tulsa's Black Wall Street
A story of Greenwood Oklahoma

But I have been talking a great deal with Percy Cook and he has been telling me wonderful things about the Army. With the wisdom, courage and heart that you have taught me, I feel fully prepared to leave home. I want to join the Army and I want to see more of the world. Now I am of age to join the Army and I would like to have your permission."

Hezekiah's answer was short but to the point. "Easy, I will support you no matter what you decide, but as you said you are of age. You have my permission to join the Army son, but then again you never really needed it."

Tulsa's Black Wall Street
A story of Greenwood Oklahoma

Chapter 7

It took a couple months, but Easy had finally made arrangements to sign up in the Army. On the day before he was to depart, Easy was a bundle of nerves. The night before leaving home as an adult, his anticipation had him charged. While the rest of his family was embracing dreams, Easy was tossing and turning. He just lay there staring at the bare ceiling. The room was dark, he was undisturbed, the bed was perfect, but no matter how hard he tried, Easy couldn't fall asleep. When he was finally able to doze off, Easy woke up several times. Each time he would wake, it was not for long, but long enough to break his sleep into un-refreshing chunks. He opened his bedroom window to enjoy a cool breeze and to hear nature's symphony. It was a rarity for that time of year, but crickets were chirping. Before finally succumbing to sleep, he puzzled why the crickets were so active that time of year. He also wondered why it was that he could often hear these creatures, but could rarely see them.

As he rose the following morning his mother had already prepared breakfast.

Tulsa's Black Wall Street
A story of Greenwood Oklahoma

Immediately upon sitting in his chair, Easy's mother served him an enormous platter of food. With butterflies in his stomach and his head buzzing with the day's possibilities, there was no way on earth he could eat a bite; not to mention an entire plateful. He turned down the food, but accepted a glass of water. While waiting to leave, he took several small sips. Looking around he kept thinking how the pain he carried in his chest was inexplicable. Over the years Easy would often imagine leaving home and seeing the world. But now he could almost hear the ghost of his childhood whimper in the sharp breeze of fall. He had no idea that leaving home was so surprisingly hard. There were so many memories, and now all of them were balled up in Easy's chest. Easy would always treasure his childhood memories, but he had grown up and life moved on. Finally, the time had come. Easy could feel his pulse pounding in his temples as he stood from the chair. Because his legs were shaky Easy walked carefully toward his mother fearing that he may trip. He hugged her lovingly, bathing in her warmth and the smell of lye from her freshly laundered clothing.

In his mother's arms, Easy felt safe and his worries always seemed to disappear; like rain on summer earth.

Tulsa's Black Wall Street

A story of Greenwood Oklahoma

As he stepped back from her, teary eyed his mother said, "Seeing you grow up and go away is bittersweet for me. Even though I want to hold you and keep you by my side I know it's the best for you to go." With that she handed Easy some food that she had prepared for his trip. She had prepared corn meal dumplings and venison and placed it in a gunnysack. He thanked his mother, kissed her on the cheek and picked up his beaten leather satchel by its frayed straps. The satchel contained everything that Easy owned in the world. Bidding farewell to his family, Easy's father took him to the Beaver, Meade and Englewood Railroad train depot.

The train was running late and there was a numbing quiet on the platform. Hezekiah broke the awkward silence saying, "Son, I honestly don't know what kind of parting this is. By that I mean as you make off to a new adventure it's possible that we will walk on diverging paths forever. Perhaps you will come back to Greenwood and perhaps you won't. All I know for certain is that I love you and am truly proud of you. Know that no matter what, my door is always open to you. Also know that I would still move heaven and earth for you. As your father I am obligated to nurture and care for you, but I am not obligated to love you.

Tulsa's Black Wall Street

A story of Greenwood Oklahoma

But I do love you and always will; no matter what." About that time a raucous, metallic shriek heralded the arrival of the iron carriage. With a firm grip Hezekiah shook his son's hand and said, "Have a safe trip and take care." Easy was moved. He knew Hezekiah to be honest to a fault and it was against his nature to deceive. Easy learned as a child that whatever Hezekiah wanted to say, he just told you straight. He didn't try to sugar-coat the truth or bargain it. He always seemed to know the significance of things and the right thing to say. At this moment his father chose the right words. He was not only showing Easy love, but he was also showing respect. He was looking at Easy more as a peer.

As it screeched to a halt, the train's doors reluctantly opened with assistance from a stocky station guard. The man stepped onto the depot platform and shouted "All Aboard….All Aboard", while simultaneously announcing all scheduled stops. Just stepping up to the train, made an increasingly nervous Easy breathe more shallow and rapidly.

Before boarding the train Easy said to his father, "I know that the bond that we share will keep us together although we will be far apart.

Tulsa's Black Wall Street

A story of Greenwood Oklahoma

But right now I have to go and find my own way in this world. Don't think of my leaving as a sign of disrespect or that I don't appreciate all of your sacrifices. Please understand that it means I love you all the more. You have taught me well and I promise to make you proud of me. Good bye father."

Shortly after Easy took his seat on the train, the iron wheels scraped against the track rails. As the wheels began to turn, the train lurched forward. Once underway the train slowly picked up speed shaking from side to side. As an optimist, Easy did not know exactly what to expect from Army life or how he would react to it, but he was excited and now on his way. Easy took his seat in an open window coach, located in the colored section. Although the blowing breeze was not exactly cold, he was trembling. His stomach shifted uneasily and a muscle twitched uncontrollably at the corner of his eye. He tapped his foot nervously while staring out of the coach car window. Easy knew that in order to get through any of life's journeys, he only needed to take one step at a time. But he also knew that he had to keep on stepping. Hypnotically, as the train rocked him back and forth, Easy closed his eyes and was eventually lulled to sleep.

Tulsa's Black Wall Street

A story of Greenwood Oklahoma

He was awakened by the train whistle as they approached the Houston railway station depot. Every journey has an end and the moment Easy had waited for was close at hand. As the train came to a stop Easy's eyes curiously wandered at the unusual activity that was going on outside. Noises were in full swing and there was a lot of traffic. There was also a uniformed man standing in front of four teams of mule-drawn wagons yelling as recruits departed the train. Easy stared in amazement as the man in the green uniform, sternly barked orders in a no nonsense manner. Judging from the man's appearance, he was certainly over thirty and considerably under fifty. With a well-toned physique and tattoos swirling on his forearms, he stood at least a head taller than anyone else. He looked hard and fit, like a man who could be a serviceable friend or a particularly unpleasant enemy.

As the recruits gathered on the platform there was seriousness about this man in the uniform that unnerved some standing there. Laughing to himself, Easy thought that this tongue lashing was mild to some that he had heard from the rednecks in Oklahoma. Standing there waiting to begin training at Camp Logan were approximately 100 men.

Tulsa's Black Wall Street

A story of Greenwood Oklahoma

To Easy's astonishment there was a melting pot of nationalities. There were even immigrants there who barely spoke English. Because many Southern civilians protested having blacks from other states inhabit nearby training camps, the War Department stipulated that no more than one-fourth of the trainees in any Army camp in the U.S. could be black. The uniformed man identified himself as a Drill Instructor. He informed everyone that he was, "assigned to instill good order and discipline into you lazy bums." After assigning which team wagons the recruits would ride, at what seemed at the top of his lungs, the Drill instructor screamed "Get in girls, we've got a lot of road to cover and a short time to get there!" The Drill Instructor's holler reverberated like a clap of thunder and such was his rage.

By the year 1917 the Army had invested in numerous motorized vehicles as replacements for mule-drawn wagons. However, the roads were in deplorable condition and mud was a constant companion. The mud wasn't even the rich black type that Easy was accustomed to in Oklahoma. This Texas mud was a sloppy, washed out grey, clayish type. The mud created numerous mechanical and overheating problems for the Army's motorized trucks.

Tulsa's Black Wall Street

A story of Greenwood Oklahoma

Considering the weight, transporting numerous recruits by mule was not necessarily fast, but because of the rough terrain to Camp Logan the commute was achieved with less effort and costs, than by motorized vehicles. All things considered, as troop carriers, the four-legged transport was deemed more dependable and less costly. Although the off-road performance of motorized vehicles was not all it could have been, there was little doubt in anyone's mind that the trucks would improve. As they developed and improved, these vehicles would eventually replace the horse and mule for military transport.

Upon enlistment, the recruits were advised to expect between thirty to ninety days of training at camp. The northern recruits were eager to enjoy a sunny South East Texas winter. Unfortunately, they found themselves disappointed. That year Houston faced one of the harshest winters on record. Heavy rain, snow, sleet, and extreme cold plagued the camp, which stayed muddy during most of their training. Troops lived in tents on wooden platforms and had difficulties staying warm. Most were forced to burn green wood for fuel, which gave off a lot of smoke but little heat. The day for recruits started at 5:30 a.m. when the bugler blew reveille, and ended at 11:00 p.m. with taps.

Tulsa's Black Wall Street

A story of Greenwood Oklahoma

At wake up, beds were made and everything tidy before a breakfast of overcooked egg and toast. The training days were consistent. The days promised rain, cold, mud, and tomorrow promised more of the same. Every man in the army was trained to obey orders for even the most unconscionable acts. The Army demanded unquestioned obedience from their soldiers and to hell with the consequences. Despite the harshness, the Army presented many black soldiers, particularly those from the rural South, with opportunities unavailable to them as civilians. As soldiers these men received such benefits as remedial education, basic health care and an eye popping $21.00 monthly pay. There were some who did not see that kind of money in six months. Weekends provided free time and recreation for the men. Unlike their white counterparts, blacks were unable to safely frequent Houston because of a black mutiny months earlier. The all-black 3rd Battalion, 24th Infantry – a unit of the famed Buffalo Soldiers was posted in Houston to guard the construction of Camp Logan. Houston was fully under Jim Crow, and while many soldiers were from the south, (they had previously been posted in Columbus, New Mexico where Jim Crow laws had not been enforced), and expected equal treatment given they were serving in the army.

Tulsa's Black Wall Street
A story of Greenwood Oklahoma

The white population of Houston instead was insistent that segregation be upheld, on the basis that black Houston residents would see the soldiers being treated decently and expect decent treatment themselves. As such the soldiers were subject to racial abuse from construction workers on the site, and police harassment in the city. On August 1917, the soldiers heard a black Corporal had been killed by police. While he hadn't been killed, he had been arrested and beaten for inquiring about the arrest and beating of another black soldier arrested for participation in a craps game. Upon hearing of the supposed death, 156 black soldiers appropriated rifles and marched into town. The soldiers killed fifteen white locals (including four police officers) and wounded another dozen whites.

The restricted access to Houston however did not deter these black soldiers from relaxing and socializing during this free time. It was during one of these off-duty periods where Easy fully became aware of Willie Weathers. Willie Weathers was a recruit in his mid-twenties, short, muscular with square shoulders and extremely dark. Coming from the violent streets of Harlem New York, Willie appeared to have a chip on his shoulder. He was tough and had the swagger of someone you didn't want to lock eyes with, let alone cross.

Tulsa's Black Wall Street

A story of Greenwood Oklahoma

It was rumored among recruits that Willie had been a numbers runner, pimp, drug dealer and had even been involved in burglaries. The word was that Willie joined the Army to get out of New York quickly because he was under suspicion for three murders. On the surface it appeared to Easy that Willie had no redeeming qualities, but Willie didn't give a damn what anyone thought of him. Willie had a violent temper and seemed to have a special dislike for southerners. He called all recruits from the south, "Country Bammas". The only thing Willie hated worse that a Country Bamma was white people. Willie once said that if he saw a white person on fire he would not piss on him to put the fire out. As an affable person, Easy kept mostly to himself. He was ambivalent toward Willie; He didn't necessarily interact with Willie and Willie didn't interact with him.

One day at dinner Willie had drawn a good deal of attention from a fellow recruit named Larry Lee. Larry had been boasting all morning to fellow recruits about how he was going to "take that damn bully down." Larry was still smoldering because he had lost all of his money to Willie shooting craps. He was far from happy about losing money that had taken him a month to earn.

Tulsa's Black Wall Street

A story of Greenwood Oklahoma

Larry had planned to send that money home, to North Carolina, to help support his mother and sister. Willie had heard of the threats and was itching for a fight. Loud talking Larry, Willie said, "I hear you mad at me Bamma. I don't think you got the balls. Fight me and you know I'll win; or maybe you like gambling?" About that time Willie began flicking peas at Larry. The peas were the size of rabbit poop, the color of snot and tasted like crap. Flick. Flick. Flick went the peas. Larry pretended to ignore Willie by keeping his head down and eating his food while fixating on a spot on the table. Willie continued…Flick. Flick. Flick went more peas.

Suddenly striking like a cobra, one of the peas met its mark hard against Larry's head. Angry, Larry jumped up, turned and rocketed forward until his face was an inch from Willie's. Clenching his fist, a vein popped out of Willie's forehead and faster than a cat jumping out of ice-water Willie swung his arm. Larry's legs gave way and he crumbled to the ground. Easy's eyes opened like two flashlight beams and his mouth was almost too dry to speak. That was one hell of a punch. Shaking his head in disbelief, Easy could only croak out "Damn!!!"

Tulsa's Black Wall Street

A story of Greenwood Oklahoma

Just before reveille the following morning as he was returning from the outhouse, Easy noticed someone lurking around outside Willie's tent. Briskly rubbing his eyes in a desperate effort to focus he realized the person lurking was Larry Lee. Although he could not make out what it was, there was an object in Larry's hand. Like a cat fixated on its prey Easy focused his attention on Larry's actions; his curiosity building. Still angry about being knocked unconscious by Willie, fires of fury and hatred were smoldering in Larry. All night he had weighed the pros and cons of the various means available to him for exacting revenge. Willie had crossed the line and Larry was not about to forget. Larry concluded that he would not rest until Willie was beaten and he didn't mean just beaten down; he meant dead. From Larry's perspective, when it came to a fight there was no code. He was going to take Willie down by any means necessary.

Easy's instincts led him to believe this was about the fight. He also believed it to be a bad situation. Easy had no love for Willie, but a seriously violent act of retribution by Larry would be bad for all black recruits. Hoping to mediate, he decided to talk with Larry. As he headed in Larry's direction, he saw the tent flap open and Larry raise his arm. Easy rushed forward and shouted "STOP".

Tulsa's Black Wall Street
A story of Greenwood Oklahoma

Startled, Larry turned and Easy pushed him from the tent. As Larry stumbled, nearly falling to the ground he dropped the knife. Caught by surprise Larry yelled at Easy, "What the hell?" Without missing a beat Easy quickly picked up the knife, grabbed Larry by the arm and escorted him away from the tent. After insuring Larry was okay, he calmly said, "Look, I just did you a big favor whether you decide to believe it or not. Like everyone else here you know about white fear after the riot from the colored soldiers a few months back. White people have their eyes on all of us. By doing something foolish you are playing right into their hands.

Coloreds are still seen as a threat to white authority around here. If you kill Willie, you could be court-martialed, imprisoned or even worse hung. You can always get money back, but you can't get a life back. The only freedom that white people are seeking for colored people is the freedom to lock us up or kill us. Don't you realize they will hang you for murder; even if it is another colored person. In the Army you have a chance at financial freedom and a new life. Willie ain't worth losing that. Just let it go."

Tulsa's Black Wall Street
A story of Greenwood Oklahoma

Chapter 8

A part of the training, for new recruits, was trench warfare. Recruits dug many miles of zigzag trenches to duplicate ones on the battlefields in France. These trenches averaged a depth of eight feet, but some were fifteen feet deep, and some had bunkers as deep as thirty feet underground. Easy was happy to discover that Larry and Willie were nowhere near each other. Thinking the group had dodged a bullet, Easy was surprised when he looked up to see Willie heading in his direction. Willie glided coolly toward Easy like a waiter in a big city restaurant. Not sure what to expect, Easy secured a firm grip on the shovel and braced himself for the worse. Walking up to Easy, Willie asked "What's shaking country?" Still suspicious Easy responded, "The name is Easy." As their eyes met, Willie said with a smirk, "That's fair Easy. So one question; why did you step in on my behalf this morning and what are you looking for? What's your angle? Are you trying to hustle me?" Without thinking Easy said, "No angle. No hustle. I just did not want white people in colored people's business. I don't want one single thing from you.

Tulsa's Black Wall Street
A story of Greenwood Oklahoma

I see an ambush as a cowardly action and I can't stand a damn coward or cowardly act." Normally Willie's face was not readable. It was almost like he would leave his emotions in the tent daily after rising. But awkwardly Willie did seem a little taken aback by Easy's response. He narrowed his eyes, tilted his head and stared at Easy for a few moments before walking away. From that point on the relationship between Willie and Easy developed into a genuine friendship. Easy and Willie gradually became friendlier over the next several weeks and Willie did change. Willie maintained his swagger was still a drinker, gambler and had a violent temper, but he was no longer a bully.

In Early 1918 before being deployed the newly trained Army recruits were granted furlough. Willie was hesitant about returning to Harlem so Easy invited him to Oklahoma. Willie spent the next two weeks enjoying the hospitality of Easy's family and Greenwood. Initially skeptical, Willie surprisingly found himself favorably impressed by the progressive black population in Greenwood.

On the evening before their furlough ended Willie was standing outside with Easy admiring the countryside that stretched before him. The countryside was an alien world to Willie.

Tulsa's Black Wall Street

A story of Greenwood Oklahoma

Willie thanked Easy for inviting him, sharing his family and "opening his eyes." Lighting a Pall Mall cigarette Willie shared with Easy that in 1905 his parents left an Alabama sharecropping farm for New York with the desire for a better life. His parents found the new sense of freedom exciting and liberating but had to endure substandard living conditions in overcrowded neighborhoods. After arriving in New York his mother found work as a domestic and his father was hired as a laborer. His father worked as a manual laborer during construction of the New York and Harlem Railroad. Willie's father was old school and a very stern disciplinarian. When Willie was twelve years old his father kicked him out of their house for taking money from his mother's purse. Willie had to live on his own wits since twelve and did not know a normal family life as Easy had. Then, after taking a long drag from his Pall Mall Willie told Easy, "I have been on my own since twelve and I've done some things that I'm not so proud. You are the only living person that I genuinely trust. You are the only family that I know. As long as there is a breath in my body, no matter the trouble, whether you are at fault or not, I will have your back. Big or small, I am your nigger. If I get big, I will just be your bigger nigger."

Tulsa's Black Wall Street
A story of Greenwood Oklahoma

The Army had two black combat divisions, the 92nd and 93rd, made up of approximately 40,000 troops. Easy and Willie were both assigned to the 93rd Division's 369th Infantry Regiment. The 93rd Division was the first black combat troops to set foot on French soil. This Regiment which was a National Guard Unit out of New York became the most famous unit of all black troops. They were nicknamed the "Harlem Hell Fighters." The regiment first garnered notoriety for its world-class band, made up of top musicians from the United States and Puerto Rico. In 1918 Easy and Willie crossed the Atlantic together as part of this Regiment to France. Easy thought he had seen a lot in life, but there was no experience that could have prepared him for what he was about to encounter. However, Easy was a fast learner who obeyed his superiors without question, proving to be a good soldier.

Initially, black soldiers sent to Europe were forbidden from battle. Combat elements of the U.S. Army were intentionally kept completely segregated. Although technically eligible for many positions in the Army, very few blacks got the opportunity to serve in combat units. Most were limited to labor battalions.

Tulsa's Black Wall Street

A story of Greenwood Oklahoma

In the all black 369th Infantry Regiment, non-band members dug ditches, cleaned latrines, transported supplies, cleared debris, and buried rotting corpses. The largest number of black troops served as stevedores, working on the docks of Brest, St. Nazaire, Bordeaux, and other French port cities.

Black soldiers would often work for twenty-four hours straight unloading ships and transporting men and materiel to and from various bases, ports, and railroad depots. Despite blacks being forbidden from combat by Army policy, white soldiers and officials who faced combat grew bitter at their black counterparts. In France white Army officials characterized black soldiers of the division as being of low character, rapists and spread vicious lies about blacks to French civilians. They would spread such tales as black soldiers were inhuman, uncivilized and smelly. They had tales, turning into apes at night. Department of Army leaders were not blind to the racist attitudes and internal conflicts confronting units. In an unpopular move, with some, the War Department decided to commission black officers. They reasoned black soldiers would be more likely to follow men of their own color, thereby reducing the risk of any sort of uprising.

Tulsa's Black Wall Street
A story of Greenwood Oklahoma

Similar to their enlisted brethren black officers were also singled out for racist treatment because of their status. A black officer was viewed at local levels as a threat to white authority. Blacks were now earning higher positions in the Army, but that did not necessarily mean they were getting equal treatment. While still discriminatory, the Army was far more progressive in race relations than the other branches of the military. Blacks could not serve in the Marines and could only serve limited and menial positions in the Navy and the Coast Guard. World War I was a transformative moment for black Americans. Ultimately the two black combat divisions, the 92nd and 93rd, did see battle.

Uncertain about how to effectively use black soldiers, the American Army loaned the 93rd Division to the French army. It was the only American division to serve exclusively under French command. Armed, organized, and equipped as a French unit, the 93d quickly adjusted to their new assignment. Although experiencing some difficulties like language problems, the black soldiers proved themselves worthy of acclaim. Despite having to acclimate to French methods of combat, the division's regiments performed exceptionally well.

Tulsa's Black Wall Street

A story of Greenwood Oklahoma

Black American troops also interacted well with North and West African soldiers serving in the French military. Serving and working closely with their African counterparts expanded the black soldier's sense of identity and belonging.

Black soldiers also received a warm welcome from French military and civilians. The French, unlike white troops of the American army, exhibited little overt racism. The rigors of combat and manual labor challenged the black soldier's physical and emotional stamina. Blacks were expected to do their part and they proved to be ferocious in showing remarkable pride during battles. Despite inadequate training and racial discrimination, the division as a whole fought well beyond expectations. There were remarkably few disciplinary problems, in the black ranks considering the backbreaking burden. Blacks were steadfast despite their adversity because French soldiers and French people treated them with respect. Actually, the French nation was completely fascinated with black culture. Their travel and service in France expanded the boundaries of how black soldiers viewed the world and their place in it. Back home in America, blacks were subjected to Jim Crow and remained second-class citizens.

Tulsa's Black Wall Street
A story of Greenwood Oklahoma

However, France did not have segregation laws and blacks were admired. Interactions with local women further contributed to the image of France as a nation free of racial discrimination and uniquely committed to democratic rights. The French were also captivated by the Black Regiment's world-class band which popularized jazz and ragtime music. Both the French and some white American troops enjoyed being introduced to the rhythmic black music that, in some cases, was previously unknown to them. Blacks also took full advantage of France's night-life. Paris's right bank offered entertainment for and catered to a diverse public. Black soldiers loved the freedom and champagne-filled parties offered for them at cafés and dance halls on Paris's right bank. Service in France constituted a remarkable life experience for black servicemen. The experience was altogether improving and broadening in changing their outlook. They began seeing things from a different perspective; it was simply a matter of getting out of America. It felt similar to a tortoise retracting into its shell; the troubles of Jim Crow and racism blacks faced across the ocean had all but evaporated. One morning after a night out on the town Willie told easy, "I admit that I was a bit concerned when I found out we were being shipped overseas.

Tulsa's Black Wall Street

A story of Greenwood Oklahoma

I didn't know what was going to happen to me in France but I knew what was going to happen to me if I stayed in New York. I am happy that we came and were able to share the experience." Laughing Easy said, "Yea, after the training at Camp Logan, I feared all we would do in France was dig trenches and kill white folks, but nothing could have prepared me for life in France. I have never been so happy to be wrong. I love it here and it's too bad we don't have this type of democracy at home." Easy's words almost seemed to forecast things to come. The time in France was quickly drawing to an end.

Needing a place to train a large number of troops quickly, during the previous year, the United States government had purchased a site in North Carolina. Located in Charlotte the site occupied approximately 4,000 acres. The new training site was named Camp Greene. A large number of soldiers were assigned there for training and to work in building the Camp. Labor was required to construct buildings and build the many miles of roads, water pipes, electrical wire and weapon ranges. In late November 1918 an armistice between the Allies and Central Powers went into effect. With the armistice in effect, in early 1919 Easy and Willie departed France returning stateside.

Tulsa's Black Wall Street
A story of Greenwood Oklahoma

Easy stood on the ship and watched, with a degree of sadness, as France slowly disappeared from view. He was returning to what white people described as the "land of the free" he thought sarcastically. Easy and Willie had been reassigned to Camp Greene in North Carolina. There was a lot of things Easy could call the state of North Carolina, but "land of freedom" did not make the top 100. After the many freedoms experienced in France, Easy's return to America was bittersweet.

Dragging his duffle bag behind him Easy stepped from the ship. Immediately upon putting his foot on American soil, Easy put the bag down, crouched low to scoop up a hand full of American earth. Similar to most other black soldiers, Easy and Willie were proud of their contributions to the war effort. They reveled and justifiably took great pride in what they had achieved. They also swelled racial pride, optimistically hoping that their patriotic sacrifices would have a positive impact on race relations. At the same time, the war also generated an abrupt change in many blacks and deepened a commitment to expand the boundaries of civil rights. These blacks took the position that if America truly understood the functions of democracy and justice then America must begin to promote democracy and justice at home first of all.

Tulsa's Black Wall Street
A story of Greenwood Oklahoma

Chapter 9

Reactions after the end of World War I proved the United States had a long way to go in race relations. During World War I the military service brought thousands of black men into the army. This experience exposed many to new lands, new people, and allowed them to fight for their country. Ideally these veterans deeply believed, and in some cases demanded that America live up to the huge debt it owed blacks. However, as the black troops returned home, rather than a decrease, they faced an increase of racial tension. Black veterans were still forced to fight, quite literally, for their survival following the war. They frequently endured residential segregation, job discrimination, substandard working conditions, and the blatant hostilities of white residents. Because of their patriotic service, veterans rightfully wanted to stake their claim to democracy and the American dream. Unfortunately, what they returned home to was a daily barrage of insults, epithets, and ingratitude. There were no Jim Crow laws to be enforced in France, but in North Carolina black soldiers encountered not only segregation but also hate within the ranks.

Tulsa's Black Wall Street
A story of Greenwood Oklahoma

White soldiers who worked with them demanded and were granted separate tanks of drinking water. Adding to their frustration was a belief that the white officers who topped their ranks were doing little to stand up for them to stop the daily denigration. Viewing how racial conditions had failed to improve and the stubbornness of white racism, Easy now understood the brilliance of Greenwood. He committed himself to combat black disentrancement and decided to return back to Greenwood after his enlistment. When he got back, Easy had hopes of starting a business venture with his good friend Willie Weathers. Not wanting to take Willie for granted he proposed the idea to Willie who happily accepted.

About 30 days had passed when one morning Willie received notice that his father had passed. After many years of estrangement, Willie's mother was trying to reconcile the family. Believing his troubles with the law had diminished he decided to return. The Army cut a few months from his enlistment to grant Willie an early military discharge. Before parting Camp Greene, Willie reminded Easy of his pledge a year earlier.

Tulsa's Black Wall Street

A story of Greenwood Oklahoma

"Although I am going to try and bury the hatchet over past deeds in New York, my opinion of our relationship has not changed. You are the only living person that I genuinely trust. If you ever need me, I am there for you." With that, Willie provided Easy all his contact information where he could likely be reached. Before Willie could depart Easy had a question that he just had to know from his good friend. "We have shared a lot together and one thing I've always wondered about and I just have to ask. What caused you to take the money from your mother's purse?" With a smile he responded, "I was trying to buy a birthday gift for my father." With a heartfelt hug, Easy smiled and said, "My Man! You will always be my Ace Boon Coon." As he walked off Willie turned once more to remind Easy, "Don't ever forget, if you ever need me, I will always be there for you; right or wrong." As the weeks drug by, Easy missed his good friend Willie. However, three short months later it was Easy's turn to go home. After two years of dedication, hard work, and sacrifice, Easy was to be granted an honorable military discharge.

As he stood in front of the military officer, Easy quietly sighed in satisfied relief, letting the happiness soak right into his bones.

Tulsa's Black Wall Street
A story of Greenwood Oklahoma

His brain tingled and a quick smirk played at the corner of his lips as he stared at the discharge papers. There seemed to be no end to Easy's fascination as his eyes surveyed the papers. In bold letters there it was; his name "Corporal Ezekiel White". Easy briefly closed his eyes to savor the moment, but he never released his grip on the precious piece of paper that he held tightly in his hands. For the first time in two years there were no more uniforms, no deadlines, no schedules. He made it through the war; he was now free of the Army and he was a veteran. The end of his military obligation seemed to lift a weight from his shoulders as if an overly large child had just leapt off after a satisfying piggy back ride. Tomorrow he would be headed for home. He wanted to always remember this feeling; even until the days when he was old and gray. Now standing upright in an assertive military posture; chin up, chest out, shoulders back and stomach in, Easy raised his arm and extended the officer a proper military salute. With his mind now more relaxed, Easy's stride was lighter and carefree as he walked away.

The next morning as Easy was preparing to board his train, he stole one final glance of North Carolina. The sun was radiant, its light creeping into every corner, bathing him in a warm glow.

Tulsa's Black Wall Street
A story of Greenwood Oklahoma

Getting underway, the train jerked forward, pushing Easy back into his seat. The train chugged along to moving at a steady pace. Journeying past rambling countryside, a series of lakes and looming mountains, the train chugged along its winding track. With no two tracts the same, the changing landscape before him was a series of almost every size, shape and color. After two days of travel, Easy knew he was drawing closer to home. He was growing deliriously happy, giddy even. Every few minutes or so he would check his pocket watch, each time he found himself disappointed that it had barely changed since the last glance. He bounced on his flexing feet and rubbed his hands together. He wore the facial expression of a small child looking at an especially large present on Christmas morning. The anticipation was a nervous kind of energy. By the time the train entered Oklahoma territory, Easy was on edge. Finally, the Rail Conductor made the call that Easy had so anxiously awaited; "TULSA!!!"

As a general rule, Easy was usually calm and collected. He hid his emotions figuring his mental state was something he'd rather people figure out. However this day was different. As he stepped onto that train platform, dragging his baggage behind him, Easy glowed from the inside out.

Tulsa's Black Wall Street
A story of Greenwood Oklahoma

The smile that cracked his face hadn't been seen since boyhood. He just had a good feeling about the day, nothing that felt this right could possibly go wrong. It just couldn't. For Easy just crossing the Oklahoma state line was somehow soothing to his soul. Suddenly he heard a melodious yet familiar voice shouting, "Easy...Easy..." As Easy focuses on the direction where the voice was coming from, his mother's warm, loving face was revealed. Easy dropped his bag and broke into a run. His embrace was intense, bear like, and his big strong arms seemed very protective when wrapped around his mother's frail body. He could feel his mother's body tremble, as she cried, releasing the worry and tension of the past two long years. The world around seemed to melt as he held his mother not wanting the moment to end. Hezekiah stood there proudly smiling from ear to ear, admiring his son standing tall in his pressed Army uniform.

As Easy turned from his weeping mother to give his father a big "real man" hug, he could hear screams of joy from his siblings and relatives around him. Everyone made their way home to a celebratory dinner. Table tops were layered with the most delicious foods and delicacies capable of making anyone's mouth water. Easy indulged, eating more than he'd thought possible.

Tulsa's Black Wall Street
A story of Greenwood Oklahoma

The celebration went on into the night, everyone eating, drinking, talking, gossiping, laughing and cutting the fool like they'd all forgotten how to stand still.

Despite a full night, Easy was still in the habit of his Army morning ritual. He was up way before the day fully dressed and ready to go. A new day had come, new possibilities, a fresh page yet to be written. Outside was still as black as night, but it was his customary time to rise. Thinking he had heard a strange noise, curiously Easy stepped outside to investigate. After closing the house door he looked up, to see something half trotting toward him. "What the hell" he thought? It wasn't a dog, sheep, or cow; it was a horse. The animal had no bridle, reins or saddle but appeared docile. As the animal advanced toward Easy, while staring attentively he approached the horse carefully from his side. The horse lowered his head and continued to move toward Easy. With tenderness and kindness he spoke softly to the animal while strongly stroking the side of its body in a rhythmical fashion. A voice from behind Easy said, "You still have a way with animals." Still stroking the animal, Easy glanced around to see Hezekiah behind him. Easy wisecracked, "And you are still good at sneaking up on people."

Tulsa's Black Wall Street
A story of Greenwood Oklahoma

Smiling Hezekiah informed Easy that the horse belonged to Ed Burns. "Do you mean Emma and Joseph's father?" Easy asked. "The same" Hezekiah responded. He related that the horse had escaped the corral a few times over the past two years. Explaining further, Hezekiah said that it's not surprising, since horses were herd animals. He suggested Easy might want to return the horse later in the morning and possibly see the Burns children.

After breakfast, Easy headed toward the Burns' place with their horse in tow. The road to the Burns was a typical desolate, narrow, and loose graveled country road. As a child Easy would imagine that the road was magic and would take him anywhere he dreamed; so long as he moved onward. Everywhere he looked and every aroma took Easy back to his misspent youth. He even saw the old oak where he ran his fingers across the initials that they all had carved into the tree very long ago. Walking up to the Burns' house front door Easy knocked three times and waited. With no response, Easy was about to knock once more when he heard the door open. It was Emma. She smiled like he was a long lost friend and shook Easy's hand warmly. Her body numbed as he looked at her. With the perfect squeeze, eye contact and a small smile playing on her face, Emma was clearly pleased to see Easy.

Tulsa's Black Wall Street

A story of Greenwood Oklahoma

With a surprised stutter she asked "Where are you going Easy? What are you doing here?" Easy explained that their horse had showed up at his father's place and he was returning it to her dad. Now understanding, she let him know that her father and brother were out looking for the horse and asked him to put the horse in their barn.

Easy walked the horse to the barn and placed the animal in a stall. After securing the stall gate he turned and noticed Emma quietly standing behind him. With a voice soft-spoken and mellow Emma said "How different you are now." While Easy was putting up the horse Emma eyes were locked, silently examining every aspect of her childhood friend. She quickly observed that his shoulders were no longer those of a youth but of a man. Reflection of the day before, she could still vividly recall how good he looked in his starched and pressed uniform. That green uniform marked him as a fighter, a protector, a defender of freedom and he was barely recognizable as the Easy of a few summers ago. She thought that his chiseled body, mahogany-brown skin, curly black hair, chocolate eyes and slight mustache turned him from handsome to divine. The feelings that surfaced were not anything like those she felt for him when they were both younger.

Tulsa's Black Wall Street

A story of Greenwood Oklahoma

She watched him move, there was something of the soldier in him combined with a gentleness that made her heart reach out.

Finally speaking Emma said, "I saw you at the train depot yesterday; welcome home. Are you home for good?" Easy related how he had been discharged and had returned home with plans of starting his own business. He mentioned how he had seen enough of the world and was ready to put down some roots. Flirtatiously batting her eyes and with an inquisitiveness she asked where he had been. Explaining that he had seen several states and had even been to France she was seemingly awestruck.

She was a fully grown woman and ready to explore the entire world, see different things, hear distant languages and experience new cultures. Sounding a bit disheartened she confided that she had only seen Arkansas and Oklahoma. With her heart now pounding, before she could stop herself she asked, "I was just wondering....do you remember the last time we saw each other?" Immediately he remembered the kiss at Worley's creek but he also recalled Walter Oakley's hanging shortly afterward. Suddenly, Easy's mouth went dry as he experienced conflicting emotions. As he looked at Emma, it was readily apparent that nature had blessed her.

Tulsa's Black Wall Street
A story of Greenwood Oklahoma

He liked the way she'd let her hair fall in relaxed curls past her shoulders. With great curves and a fuller bust there was no more little Emma, she was now all woman.

He finally acknowledged remembering that unpredictably crazy kiss saying, "I'm not saying I did not like it because I did, but where does it lead us? Do you know where we are and how the people around here would have reacted had we been caught? We were playing with fire; it's not like we were in some place without Jim Crow like France." Amazed at the thought of a place without segregation she asked Easy to tell her about France. Weaving magical tales of Paris' mystical beauty, he called it a paradise. He disclosed how in France people of all colors lived and played together regardless of color without labels. He described the champagne-filled parties on the right bank, dance halls and above all how they catered to a diverse public. Emotionally, he related how service in France constituted a remarkable life experience thereby broadening his outlook on life." Easy held her undivided attention and Emma was mesmerized. Emma felt her cheeks flush and her heart pound with excitement as his stories about France filled her with wonder. In that moment she blushed ever so slightly and imagined Easy being her man.

Tulsa's Black Wall Street
A story of Greenwood Oklahoma

Her thoughts erupted into a series of bells, whistles, twists and turns all coming together to one question. She wondered how it was that a single thought could resurface long buried emotions and stir what was settled; but this thought had. Uncertain of how, Emma found the nerve to ask Easy the one question that had stimulated her interest. She asked Easy if he had been with a white woman while in France. Without hesitation, Easy responded, yes without further explanation.

Easy's intensity, honesty and gentleness was a side Emma had never seen and it nearly took her breath away. She thought back to when they were younger, remembering how shy and uncomfortable he was then. If only he knew how simply taken she was with him. As Easy looked in Emma's direction, she could feel his eyes. She silently inhaled and exhaled, hoping that his thoughts about her were good. Emma pondered how it was possible that her heart would somersault in such a way standing near Easy. His voice, his face, his serious lips and shoulder muscles were all her brain would dwell on. Finally Emma built up the nerve to tell Easy that she missed him while he was away. She had not forgotten their first kiss and regretted that it had not gone further.

Tulsa's Black Wall Street
A story of Greenwood Oklahoma

She also admitted to knowing that he was arriving and seeing him the previous day at the train depot. She witnessed him surrounded by others and wanted so much to take him by the hand and lead him away. There was a desperate desire to walk with him, talk with him and relive their lost opportunity, but there were rules of social decorum. Unprepared for such a confession, shock, concern and disbelief registered on Easy's face. He tried to be logical with her and pretended he was not interested until she softly placed her hand on his arm. Then something not only stirred in him, but it took over his thinking. Emma linked her fingers into Easy's hand and shot him a look that was all love; just the right hint of softness, a crease at the corners of her eyes. Suddenly Easy embraced Emma and held her tightly in his muscular arms. The rest of his world became an unimportant blur and Jim Crow was banished into the far recesses of his mind. The only thing that mattered was touching her more and kissing her. Emma stepped back, giving Easy a look and there was no doubting her wonderfully wicked idea.

However, remembering where they were, she realized they had been alone much too long.

Tulsa's Black Wall Street
A story of Greenwood Oklahoma

Understanding the precarious nature of their relationship they arranged to meet in secret later that evening.

Tulsa's Black Wall Street
A story of Greenwood Oklahoma

Chapter 10

True to the promise he had made to Willie, Easy worked at establishing a freight transport business. As a freight transporter, Easy's business involved physically transporting bulk commodities, merchandise goods and cargo by ground. A transport could be moving goods from a production facility to any place as designated or between two businesses. By late 1920, Greenwood boasted its own bus line, high schools, public library, hospital, drug stores, hotels, newspapers, theaters, and thirteen churches. There were also over 150 two and three story brick commercial buildings that housed clothing stores, grocery stores, cafes, rooming houses, nightclubs, and a large number of professional offices. The professional offices hosted doctors, lawyers, and dentists. The community also boasted some of the city's most elegant residential homes. These homes were of beauty and splendor; one of which belonged to Easy. With that backdrop, Easy developed a vast pool of networking contacts and operated a thriving business. Taking the chance of starting out in business was tough, but Easy accepted the challenge. It was hard work but proved to be well worth the effort.

Tulsa's Black Wall Street
A story of Greenwood Oklahoma

Over time he also used his veteran status and reputation to bring in lots of business. The war effort allowed a number of black veterans the courage to assert their rights as a citizen in holding the government accountable, and protesting racial injustice. In addition to the railroad, Easy aggressively lobbied the federal and state governments for business contracts.

Over this same period, Easy and Emma continued with their clandestine meetings. Easy finally admitted to himself what he knew all along, but it was too irrational to admit. He deeply cared for Emma and all she wanted was to be with him. She had contemplated for years about the pleasure of being with Easy, and often dreamed about the thrill of taking a chance. During his duty overseas, he never imagined that she was waiting and wanting to see her childhood friend. After that first kiss, Easy was someone that she wanted to know more than anyone else ever before. He was a guy that she could love for eternity. She thought Easy was a living work of art. His svelte, yet muscular body and his gorgeous brown skin aroused her. Her skin tingled where he touched her and she became easily aroused. One passionate look from him triggered a fire in Emma that was hotter than a thousand suns.

Tulsa's Black Wall Street

A story of Greenwood Oklahoma

April 15, 1921 was a postcard perfect day. At last spring had arrived, breathing warm winds over the desolate landscape. Easy stepped outside his home, stretched and tilted his face upward to greet the new day. It was a Friday morning and better yet it was Emma's birthday. They had planned a secluded evening and both were counting the minutes. For her part, Emma had taken a position as an elevator operator for the Drexel building in downtown Tulsa. Additionally, she had also moved from her parent's home establishing a household in the city to protect her privacy. The last thing she wanted was the prying eyes of relatives, friends and neighbors poking around too closely into her private affairs. Understanding the extreme danger, the secret lovers had also developed a sophisticated set of cues, gestures and sounds to convey signals. They had planned a romantic late evening picnic to celebrate her birthday. During childhood, the group of friends established a secret meeting place in the woods surrounding Worley's creek to avoid detection by adults. As a usual precaution Easy made an early reconnaissance of the area to assure their privacy and safety. Upon approaching the tree-line Easy noticed a horse tied up to a tree. Beside the horse tied to the tree was another horse and buckboard.

Tulsa's Black Wall Street
A story of Greenwood Oklahoma

As he crept closer, Easy could hear voices babbling like a mountain river. He recognized from their voices that it was a male and female. Beneath the talk was love, but their conversation was also one of worry. After positioning himself where he could witness without being observed, Easy watched everything. It didn't take long for him to realize that the real communication was not in their words, but the young woman's actions. She was sitting on a blanket with a young man and both were partially clothed. As she noticed the daylight began to dwindle her tensions grew. The young woman was frantically trying to dress gathering her clothing in the middle of the blanket. His clothes were hanging on nearby tree branches. The young man pleaded with the woman to not dress and attempted to coerce her into making out once more. As she raised her arm to put on her brassiere, he gave it a gentle tug as she smacked his hand away.

"I said NO!!!" she exclaimed. "I promised to be back before dark and I am already late. Poppa will know it didn't take me this long to get the medicine for his pigs and will be angry. If I don't have his package back soon he is going to scold me; at best." Like a bolt of lightning, it suddenly struck Easy. He finally recognized the young woman and realized that he knew her identity.

Tulsa's Black Wall Street

A story of Greenwood Oklahoma

The young woman was Jr.'s sister Rebecca Chase. Knowing the old man's temper, Easy understood her worry and concern. As she quickly ran her fingers through her hair and vigorously brushed off her clothing the young man hesitantly dressed. When they both finished dressing, the young couple walked into the clearing. They embraced, kissed and he patted her on the backside before departing their separate ways. After waiting a few moments to assure they would not return, Easy continued with his reconnaissance of the area.

The sun began to sink lower in the sky, with the light of day slowly draining away, giving way to the velvety dark of night. Crickets were chirping, the dusky colors were soft and restrained by the first stars in the late evening darkening night sky. The weather was gorgeous, perfect for the anticipated romantic candle lit picnic dinner. He lugged in everything for their romantic encounter, set out the cues and waited. With nothing but the trees for company Easy and Emma were afforded complete liberty for their forbidden love. Theirs was a love as obvious as the morning sun and as real as the grass. Theirs was a love of patience, enchantment and adventure. Whatever they talked of never mattered, only that they were talking and connected.

Tulsa's Black Wall Street
A story of Greenwood Oklahoma

Sitting engrossed in each other the young couple only wanted one thing; not to be judged. Savoring their stolen moments was important to them because tomorrow was not guaranteed to anyone; especially them. They were no longer children. As Easy softly ran his hand up Emma's bare arms, he sent a spark of electricity through her that jump started her heart. That night as they lay there in each other's arms, in their lover's tango, there was eroticism, love, safety, passion and danger all rolled into one. For Emma, her Easy was more addictive than any drug ever known to mankind. The afterglow of making love flowed through them as their intimate conversation quietly filled the night air, until the time to part arrived. Easy prayed for a day when God would grant him to see a time of such freedom as he had seen in France.

In France the pathways to love was granted to all, but he held out little hope for such freedom ever in the states. There was nothing novel about a rendezvous between two loving parties, but their behavior was novel, licentious and unlawful solely because they were of a different race. Easy and Emma were living in their own euphoric world however, they had to keep their joy a secret. They were unable to share their jubilation with family members or even friends.

Tulsa's Black Wall Street
A story of Greenwood Oklahoma

As the wind tousled her auburn hair Emma said to Easy, "If they're going to hang you for loving me, they'd best be tying two nooses to that tree. What we have done, we did together, and if our love is a capital offence; I'm ready to die alongside you." Since children he always liked to hear Emma talk. In that romantic setting under the stars he drank in her words like a fine wine. She always knew the right things to say and it was just what he needed to hear. He watched her like she had the stars in her eyes and wanted to wrap her in his arms and never let go. Turning to her with his trademark warm eyes he told Emma, "So long as you're by my side, my sweet Emma, the rest of the world can go screw themselves." Regardless of their feeling there was still legislated segregation. People were observant and could easily pick-up on a familiar laughter, an improper touch, misplaced smile or a gaze that lingered too long when they parted. Easy was the one, he always was. However, they could never be too careful. Despite it being nearly 1 a.m., with a practiced nonchalance each walked away from the other, both feeling the wrench of parting. It was better to always be on guard and not become unnecessarily careless.

When Rebecca finally arrived home that evening her fears about returning home late were validated.

Tulsa's Black Wall Street
A story of Greenwood Oklahoma

Before she even entered the home, Rebecca could hear her father in a rage. Directing his rage toward Kenneth Junior screaming, "YOU'RE NOT A MAN!!! YOU'RE A FAILURE!!! YOU"RE A GOD DAMNED LOSER!!! Everything that I have worked for is squandered by you damn ill-raised children. Your trifling mammy ain't much better. Look at this place, it is a God damn mess." Kenneth Sr. was a bit of a drinker and his fury burned with a dangerous intensity. When his anger came, it was unleashed without thought of consequence.

That is how Kenneth Junior got his insecurities and how Rebecca and her mother got their bruises and scars. As Rebecca walked through the door, unable to escape his attention, Kenneth Sr. directed his wrath toward her. Running his calloused hand through his close cropped hair, Kenneth Sr. fixed a stare on Rebecca and snarled, "Where the hell have you been all this time?" Calmly she tried to remind him that she stopped to pick up the pig medicine he had requested, on her way home from a church meeting. About to speak he began, "what?" but inexplicably he stopped in mid-sentence. Without a word he stood motionless studying Rebecca like an animal studying its prey. Hooking his thumbs into the loops of his worn jeans, Kenneth Sr. dropped his gaze to the floor.

Tulsa's Black Wall Street

A story of Greenwood Oklahoma

He inspected Rebecca from feet to head, sizing her up. Without warning his hand cracked across Rebecca's face, snapping her head back with a force that slammed backward into the door behind her. "Do you take me for some kind of a fool?" he asked. She staggered clutching her face. With her eyes watering and black dots covering her vision she begged, "What is it poppa? Please don't hit me again. Please poppa." "I am not blind. I can see that dirt stain on your dress and that whisker burn on your cheek. You little tramp; who have you been with?"

Just below her eye was a small cut where the ring had caught her causing Rebecca to weep in pain. With tears starting to flow and while trying to control the bleeding she swore that he was mistaken. Due to the combination of alcohol and his continued rage her denials only served to further infuriate Kenneth Sr. His rage now held all the power of a raging wildfire. One could almost see the flames blazing in his eyes, ready to ignite anything that he came in contact with. His temper was like dynamite and once the sparks ignited there was very little time to duck and cover. In his fury Kenneth Sr. lashed out at Rebecca. All of a sudden, everything went black. Her vision blurred as he slapped her hard with his big meaty paw.

Tulsa's Black Wall Street
A story of Greenwood Oklahoma

With her mother and Jr. witnessing the assault, her father began striking Rebecca repeatedly and harder with each blow. Rebecca let out a strangled scream. She could feel and taste the blood from her tongue she had just bitten through. With her eyes swollen over and bloody spit drooling from her mouth, in a sick manner Kenneth Sr. seemed to derive some sense of pleasure in his brutal assault.

As she lay battered and crumpled on the floor with bruises everywhere and trying to defend against his continuing reign of blows, her brain contemplated a way out. Her fear and pain generated an abundance of thoughts of how to avoid the physical attack, leaving no room for anything else. She thought, "If I tell him that I was with Little Freddy Midkiff, I will have to confess everything. If I try to cover up that we made out by telling part of the truth, it might come out anyway. If he finds out that I lied he will certainly see red and become even more violent." Wailing in pain, Rebecca decided to lie, screaming "IT WAS A COLORED MAN! IT WAS A COLORED MAN!! A colored man tried to attack me." At that moment, Kenneth Sr. stopped the fierce onslaught asking, "A nigger tried to attack you?" There was a self-loathing in having to lie but Rebecca was now in survival mode. It was either a colored man or her.

Tulsa's Black Wall Street

A story of Greenwood Oklahoma

Words flew from her mouth that she did not want to say but she did, "Yes papa, a colored man tried to grab me. He jumped out of the woods near the North Bridge blocking the roadway stopping the horse. He grabbed me and pushed me to the ground but I fought him off. I brushed myself off the best that I could. I also didn't want to say anything because I knew you would be mad." Oddly Rebecca's confession appeared to temporarily dampen his brutality. She knew instantly from his reaction and the look in his eyes that her false confession had hit their mark. Black people were the object of his hatred and he hungered for their destruction. His rancor had blackened Kenneth Sr.'s soul with hate and had become central to his person. He almost seemed happy that his daughter was accosted providing him a legitimate reason to exact revenge.

Rebecca glanced over at her father's face through swollen eyes. He just stood there stony faced with hard staring eyes and clinched fists. Suddenly he slammed both fists down hard, breaking a small table. As expected Kenneth Sr. was in a rage, but oddly enough his rage somehow seemed unusually controlled. It was almost as if Rebecca's confession was what he wanted. This was like a bad dream and she was unable to wake.

Tulsa's Black Wall Street
A story of Greenwood Oklahoma

Based on an insight to her father's world of hate, her intuition led Rebecca to be fearful of what he might do next. As it turned out her gut feelings about what might happen proved to be correct.

Tulsa's Black Wall Street

A story of Greenwood Oklahoma

Chapter 11

After all the dysfunctional commotion within the household that night, Kenneth Sr. sent Rebecca to bed. Lying in bed restlessly, she wanted so much to melt onto her cotton mattress, but there was tenseness from physical and mental pain. In Rebecca's battle with sleeplessness, she would occasionally drift off to sleep. However, more than the physical pain, her mental trauma made sleep worse than being awake. During brief bouts with sleep, she had nightmares visualizing the physical assault over and over again; she would then awake in panic. The nightmares were like a vicious cycle. It was like when she was asleep, there were nightmares of the house burning and she couldn't dowse it. Other than more water, the only thing that could save her from the nightmare was sleep. But the demons of her lies had created a mental trauma hindering a peaceful sleep. Rebecca wanted so much to find peace behind her closed eyelids unfortunately she had created her own prison. All she desired was to be absorbed into the untroubled peace of darkness that the night had always provided.

Tulsa's Black Wall Street

A story of Greenwood Oklahoma

Instead of peace she found only the chaos of torment resulting from her lies that she was forced to endure. Desperately she wanted sleep, but for hours she lay there restless tormented by her conscious. The early morning outside was still black as night, but Kenneth Sr. was fully dressed and shouting at Rebecca venomously. Jerking her up, he said it was time to rise, demanding that she dress and get ready to go. A bit afraid, she timidly asked where they were going. In a boisterous manner, he responded "We are going to see the Sheriff."

While the old weather beaten and trusty truck slowly chugged down the dirt country road, Rebecca's brain was a violent whirl. She was still rationalizing the utter pandemonium she knew would result from her lies. However as she stared in her father's direction, he seemed not to notice. Her father was happily smoking from his corn cob pipe. In that instant she knew that he had made up his mind. There would be bloodshed in the colored community. At this stage even telling the truth would be pointless, so she prayed that God would forgive her for the sin of what she was about to do.

Tulsa's Black Wall Street

A story of Greenwood Oklahoma

Although his visit to the Sheriff's office was unannounced, as Kenneth Sr. pulled up to the jail a number of people had already assembled. They were all white, armed, carrying confederate stars and bars flags. As Rebecca stepped from the truck, aside from the bruises, she was white as chalk. Her darkened eyes and swollen mouth were frozen wide open in an expression of stunned surprise. She was wearing a frayed wrap over skirt, threadbare high neck blouse, a ragged ponytail, with loose hair falling over her features and walking with an obvious limp. Obviously battered looking, in avoiding eye contact, she stared straight ahead trying not to notice them at all. As Rebecca's steps faltered, the armed assailants stood wild eyed, nostrils flaring, looking as if the blood had drained from their faces. Some held hands over their mouths and began shaking their heads as in disbelief.

Kenneth Sr. presented Rebecca to Sheriff Champ with a badly bruised body, severely battered face, swollen eyes and still wincing in pain. Belligerently he announced, "Sheriff I want you to take a look at what one of your niggers did to my little girl. I want to know what you plan to do." Politely the Sheriff allowed Rebecca to sit and patiently requested that he be allowed to interview her.

Tulsa's Black Wall Street
A story of Greenwood Oklahoma

After explaining the process he asked her several questions including: Whether or not she knew the attacker; the element of force; and the issue of consent. He asked for a detailed physical description including, skin color, clothing, tattoos, facial features, identifying marks, distinctive walk, odors, etc. He also requested that she identify the crime scene. Rebecca was not very skillful in the art of deception. She had deliberately concocted a chain of lies to cover up her secret, but numerous questions resulted in multiple inconsistencies. As a competent and savvy investigator, the half-truths and various deviations left Sheriff Champ skeptical of Rebecca's version of events. When he completed the interview, the Sheriff accompanied Rebecca and her father to see the medical doctor. Sheriff Champ and one of his deputies conducted an examination of the site where Rebecca alleged she was attacked. Despite conflicting accounts and the physician's examination of Rebecca found no evidence of rape or assault he investigated the complaint. Desiring immediate action, Kenneth Sr. grew frustrated with the Sheriff for actually conducting a legitimate investigation.

Tulsa's Black Wall Street

A story of Greenwood Oklahoma

Showing his dissatisfaction with the perceived lack of urgency, Kenneth Sr. confronted the Sheriff. Challenging the Sheriff's methods, he asked, "Is that it? Is that all you're gonna do is ask questions? I want to know what else you plan to do. She told you that the nigger did it and nigger is another word for guilty. If you can't control your niggers maybe you need to be replaced. Me and my boys; we know how to take care of them animals." In an effort to circumvent trouble, the Sheriff told Kenneth Sr. that the investigation was being conducted "in accordance with the law." Mistrustful and suspicious of the Sheriff's loyalty Kenneth Sr. responded, "Who's law; Nigger law? Do you want to keep your job? You'd best remember which side your bread is buttered on." Kenneth Sr. returned home and walked through the door with a smoldering stare into the abyss. Jr. could feel his father's evil thoughts as they all gnarled together poisoning his mind. Jr. knew it would not be long before his twisted mind would seek blood.

That same afternoon Easy received a cryptic telephone call at work. The call was from Jr. Chase who insisted that he needed to speak with Easy on an urgent matter. Easy still remembered Jr.'s involvement in the hanging of Walter Oakley, but he also knew that Jr. was not mean spirited.

Tulsa's Black Wall Street

A story of Greenwood Oklahoma

They agreed to meet at Easy's home around 7:30 that evening. That evening, Easy had just sat down at his kitchen table when he heard a knock on his door. Looking at his watch, he saw the time was 6:55. As he got up and walked toward the door he thought, "Damn, whatever Jr. has to tell me must be urgent for him to show up this early." As Easy opened the door expecting to chastise Jr., suddenly words left him. All his thoughts about what Jr. wanted and of being disturbed early had been erased from his mind as he gawked at the person standing in front of him. Every muscle of Easy's body froze before a grin finally crept onto his face, as he asked rhetorically, "WILLIE?" A small smile played on Willie's lips as he got a kick at the shock that registered on Easy's face. Initially Willie wore a face like he was expecting Easy to be angry about the lack of contact since leaving the Army but that anger just didn't exist. As he hugged his good friend, all Easy had for Willie was love. Willie's worry was only misplaced guilt because he had once run afoul of the law. "What's shaking?" Willie asked. Showing every tooth, Easy responded, "Ain't nothing jumping but the peas in the pot, and they wouldn't be jumping if the water wasn't hot."

Tulsa's Black Wall Street
A story of Greenwood Oklahoma

Inviting him inside, Easy was happy to see Willie but was blind to his natural tendency to behave in a particular way. He asked Willie, "I'm glad to see you brother. So tell me what brings you to Greenwood?" Willie was always as cool as a polar bear's toenails. Glancing over at Easy, the corners of his lips fighting a smile and his eyebrows slightly raised, Willie said he was trying to avoid unnecessary harassment. "Unnecessary harassment", Easy asked? Willie explained, "Well there was this misunderstanding between me and this four-flusher over a debt. You know me Easy, I had to bust a cap in him." "You shot someone again; and left town" Easy asked? "Well…yes if you put it that way. But I promise you Easy, he deserved it; and I didn't cancel his stamp." Willie said. Shaking his head Easy said, "Boy what am I going to do with you? Do you want anything to eat or drink?" Now smiling broadly Willie asked, "Do you have any Gin? You know what I always say. Drink gin cause it ain't no sin." As Willie sat down, Easy walked into another room. Just as Easy walked off, someone knocked on the front door. Easy yelled back and asked Willie to get the door. Upon opening the door, there was a white man standing there who appeared to be taken aback by Willie's presence.

Tulsa's Black Wall Street
A story of Greenwood Oklahoma

Noticing that the white man appearing rattled, a suspicious Willie reached for his gun and asked, "What's up Snowflake?" Easy overheard Willie and hurried back into the room. Easy told Willie he was expecting Jr. as he let him into the house. Taking a deep breath Easy said to Willie, "Damn man, your social skills need some serious work."

Knowing Jr. since childhood, when he walked into the house, Easy felt that he was troubled. Easy was about to find that a rude awakening awaited him and he too would soon be troubled. As Jr. sat down Easy observed that his footsteps were unsure, he was noticeably jittery and biting his nails. Easy asked Jr. to take a deep breath and questioned him about what was so urgent. Jr. reminded Easy that he owed him a lot and wanted to warn him. He told Easy about the episode between his sister and his father; and the false confession of an assault. Describing his father as an unscrupulous manipulator, he explained how Kenneth Sr. put on an act of caring for his daughter when he actually did not give a damn. He believed his father was using the situation to exact some kind of aggressive action and violence against blacks.

Tulsa's Black Wall Street

A story of Greenwood Oklahoma

He warned Easy that Kenneth Sr. had threatened the Sheriff and his father did not make idle threats. Jr. was certain there would be bloodshed after discovering the men his father had contacted. Easy disclosed that he had seen Rebecca that night and identified Freddy Midkiff as the man she was with. Jr. had suspected all along that she was with Freddie. After Jr. departed Easy immediately went to provide his father a heads-up and to seek guidance; with Willie in tow.

As he had so accurately forecasted to Easy, Kenneth Sr.'s actions were exactly as Jr. foretold. The following morning, Kenneth Sr. arrived at the alleged crime scene with a confusing carousel of people with no good intention. It was an armed mob of approximately 20 dangerous-looking white men with bloodhounds. As Kenneth Sr. removed a glove, he raised a bottle of whiskey to his lips. After a sip, he replaced the cap and handed it off. The rest of the mob was also drinking whiskey, making nooses and appealing to racial pride. Simultaneously, back in Tulsa, Sheriff Champ was visited by an attorney. Based on Easy's conversation with his father and other city leaders, the Greenwood NAACP hired a defense counsel in the event a black was detained. The attorney reminded Sheriff Champ of due process and his responsibilities under the law.

Tulsa's Black Wall Street
A story of Greenwood Oklahoma

The NAACP didn't want a questionable complaint to adversely impact black citizens in an abusive way. Despite the questionable credibility of the complainant and no evidence of assault there was grave concern about mob mentality and their disregard for black lives, liberty or property. They wanted to impress upon Sheriff, his obligations under the Fifth and Fourteenth Amendments to the Constitution. During the meeting Sheriff Champ was made aware of the mob that was out looking for the suspect.

Concerned they had a valid concern, after meeting with the NAACP attorney, Sheriff Champ and two deputies pursued the mob. Nearly three hour later, he tracked the armed assailants to the home of Isaac Washington. Despite Isaac's struggle to explain that they had the wrong person, the mob seized, beat and tied his hand behind him. The Sheriff reminded Kenneth Sr. that Isaac was nearing seventy five years old, in poor health and with a lame foot. Kenneth Sr. contended "The dogs led us directly to this house. Isaac may act and pretend to be a good and trustworthy boy, but the hounds do not lie. He ain't confessed what he did yet, but he will; or die."

Tulsa's Black Wall Street

A story of Greenwood Oklahoma

Other than his two deputies, the Sheriff had nothing else to protect him but one shotgun, the hand guns they carried, his words and a badge. The law had been good enough in the past, but with Kenneth Sr.'s stoking the fires of racism and the combination of whiskey, Sheriff Champ hoped that it would be good enough this time. To his advantage the Sheriff knew these men personally and understood their strengths and weaknesses. He listened to their gripes, patiently listening while they tried to make their case and he rarely interrupted. Without pushing too hard, Sheriff Champ stressed how the principle of law and order was to preserve good public order. He was firm, reasonable and principled. Despite the skepticism of some, Isaac was handed over to the Sheriff.

Tulsa's Black Wall Street
A story of Greenwood Oklahoma

Chapter 12

Isaac Washington was placed in custody and in his defense the NAACP attorney emphatically denied guilt and vehemently protested his arrest. They also referred to the fact that he had been arrested, yet no charges had been brought against him. In Isaac's defense there was advanced age, frail health and no physical evidence linking him to the crime, or anywhere near the crime scene. Because the physician's examination found no evidence of assault and the numerous inconsistencies in Rebecca's account, Sheriff Champ knew the NAACP attorney's assertion of Isaac's innocence was likely correct. However the Mayor and his council came under "considerable pressure" from white residents to do something. Presuming Isaac was guilty, white people were appalled at the audacity of a black man accosting a white woman. White citizens demanded swift justice from the Mayor. After forceful persuasion from white citizens and council members alike, the Mayor acquiesced. The Mayor coerced Sheriff Champ to charge Isaac with assault of a white woman and demanded that the city Attorney adjudicate.

Tulsa's Black Wall Street

A story of Greenwood Oklahoma

The white townspeople grew infuriated by what they perceived as an attempt to delay a speedy trial, and a threat of mob violence quickly developed. Fanning the flames of hate, the Ku Klux Klan was proactive in pushing their own narrative of events. As word of the crime spread, the degree of depravity, perversion and moral corruption in details grew with each retelling. The obscenity of it all was shocking and whites in Tulsa demanded an immediate trial of Isaac. Bowing to pressure a trial date was set for two days later. There was a clear dichotomy of opinion between blacks and whites concerning the ramifications of Isaac's trial. Black people were skeptical of the justice system. They saw courts as an unjust mechanism to fortify the political ideology of white supremacy and further disenfranchise blacks. They viewed Isaac as a scape goat and wanted to see him freed. White citizens regarded the trial as a reinforcement of Americanism. They embraced Protestantism as an essential component of their civilized society and called for strict morality. The Ku Klux Klan preached purification, wanting to restore racial subordination in every aspect of society.

Tulsa's Black Wall Street

A story of Greenwood Oklahoma

The Klan demanded stronger enforcement of oppressive laws, characterizing all blacks as barbaric. For whites, exacting justice required that Isaac be found guilty and pay for his crime.

On the day of Isaac's trial, the crowd at the courthouse was massive. Excitement buzzed through the charged air. White citizens gathered seeking vengeance whereas, showing disdain for the sham trial, black citizens gathered in disbelief. Reflecting the social turmoil, in Tulsa, Ku Klux Klan members created their own unique spectacle. Led by Kenneth Sr., a number of Klansmen paraded through Tulsa streets to the courthouse in full robes and pointed hoods; many on robed horses. They dismounted from their horses with infectious grins, patting one another on the back. Even in the summer sun, blacks shivered as the Klansmen received a spontaneous outpouring of emotion from the assembled crowd. It was a scene from their worst nightmare. Most raised their eyebrow and just shrugged it off, as the disbelief was off the charts.

The courtroom was a two story building. White people sat on the main floor while black people were only allowed to sit in the balcony. Because of the large crowd the building filled quickly. For security reasons Sheriff Champ, Isaac, the NAACP Defense Attorney and prosecuting Attorney were already in the courthouse.

Tulsa's Black Wall Street

A story of Greenwood Oklahoma

Upon his entrance, the bailiff addressed the open court. He directed the crowd's attention to the front and ordered for all to stand in announcing the judge. After taking his seat, the judge directed everyone to be seated and ordered both legal counsels to approach the bench. As the judge was speaking to both attorneys, Deputy Letchworth rushed in and whispered in Sheriff Champ's ear. Sheriff Champ immediately approached the judge's bench, where a very animated exchange took place between all parties. Shortly afterward everyone returned to their respective seats and the judge made an announcement to the entire courtroom.

In a conciliatory tone he asked for understanding and calm from all. He then announced "there had been a fire bombing at three colored churches with the possibility of multiple deaths. This unexpected occurence will require our police and fire departments full attention. In the spirit of transparency, so colored people can attend, I will delay this hearing for one day." Then looking in the direction of the balcony he directed the blacks assembled to go check on their loved ones and property. Sheriff Champ handed custody of Isaac to Deputy Letchworth. The deputy was directed to place Isaac back in detention, secure the jail and stay there until everyone returned.

Tulsa's Black Wall Street

A story of Greenwood Oklahoma

Bloodthirsty, and showing no moral principles, the Klan unscrupulously incited the crowd with bigoted rhetoric. Kenneth Sr. suggested that "the Ku Klux Klan restore order in our community. We will defend to the death white female virtue. Them boys are rapists and want nothing more than having access to our white women. Why just last month we caught a nigger boy peeping through a window watching a white woman tinkle; Hung him!! Them niggers in Little Africa are getting awful bold and uppity. There is nothing but immorality there; niggers drinking booze, taking dope and lusting for our white women. I will tell you right now, that nigger sitting in jail don't need a trial; he needs to hang." Losing all self-control the maddened mob stormed the jailhouse, broke into the cell where Isaac was incarcerated and dragged him outside. The mob first beat, then hanged Isaac from a telegraph pole near the courthouse, and finally shot his body repeatedly. The Klan dragged Isaac's body to the alleged scene of Rebecca's assault. His head was cut from his body and displayed on a pole that was stuck into the ground, and finally his body was burned.

Upon hearing the news of Isaac's death, blacks in Greenwood were justifiably enraged and rejected Tulsa's racist regime.

Tulsa's Black Wall Street

A story of Greenwood Oklahoma

They bitterly complained that the city had failed to provide due process to protect all of its citizens equally. Isaac's murder combined with the nitroglycerin bombing of three churches deepened their commitment to combat white violence. The combination of kerosene and nitroglycerin caused a raging inferno killing 5 adults and 2 children. The prosperity, wealth and prominence of Greenwood had created a feeling of angst among the white residents of Tulsa. Black accomplishments and affluence was contrary to the Klan's ideology that white people were superior; which they perceived as bold disobedience. Now many young black men were returning home from the War believing, as a veteran, they had earned full rights as a citizen. Black Americans optimistically hoped that their patriotic sacrifices would have a positive impact on race relations and expand the boundaries of civil rights.

Black people wanted to stake claim to democracy demanding that America live up to its promise of a better life for black people. During war, the national rhetoric declared that America joined the war to make the world safe for democracy, but for black Americans who were being terrorized and denied their constitutional rights, that battle cry now rang hollow.

Tulsa's Black Wall Street
A story of Greenwood Oklahoma

The fire- bombing and hanging were the final straw and blacks were fed up. Black veterans who were experienced with firearms and combat were prepared to take up arms, even if it meant outright armed rebellion. They wanted to relive the experience of life they enjoyed in France. They were determined to no longer endure random hostilities from whites or the indignities and injustice of Jim Crow. Rhetorically they asked can it be justice to be born into such pain? Can it be justice to live in such violence? Blacks were adamant that change was coming; it had to. For their part, blacks were prepared to sacrifice everything. They reasoned that whatever came was destiny, this is what the past three hundred years had been building towards. They saw their only recourse and rallying cry as, "change or die!"

To further complicate the situation, oil production was booming but overall Tulsa was suffering an economic slump that increased unemployment. Greenwood on the other hand was flourishing and enjoying rapid economic growth. Despite Tulsa's economic woes, Greenwood was still creating jobs and producing revenue. Blacks were relocating to Greenwood in large numbers and struggling to keep pace with the increased housing demands. The wealth of blacks was even more impressive.

Tulsa's Black Wall Street

A story of Greenwood Oklahoma

Six of Greenwood's black families owned their own planes. Greenwood's success made the city ripe for white animosity against black economic progress. The Ku Klux Klan equated improvements in Greenwood's economy and working conditions as a communistic threat. Whites were now resentful that blacks were no longer willing to passively accept second-class citizenship. White Americans, especially the Ku Klux Klan, feared that Greenwood's demand of respect for black residents would "snow-ball". If Greenwood was successful it would encourage other blacks to resist Jim Crow segregation and other racially oppressive social customs.

The Ku Klux Klan displayed a narrow-minded resistance to any change. In protest to black equality, the Klan angrily vented describing blacks as predisposed to crime and in need of social control. They were determined to reestablish the natural order of white superiority at all costs. Due to false assumption of black criminality, the Ku Klux Klan justified the use of deadly violence. On May 29th 1921 as the long shadows of evening dissolved into the darkness of night, Sheriff Champ sat alone in the solitude of his home. He sat there knee deep in silence, unable think straight, his foot tapping up and down, with his head buzzing with possibilities.

Tulsa's Black Wall Street
A story of Greenwood Oklahoma

There was a fragile peace between Tulsa and Greenwood residents, but tempers were boiling. The Ku Klux Klan was aggressively pushing a narrative and its logic was beginning to take root with whites. The darkness worried Sheriff Champ as his imagination supplied many fears. He was the rabbit, hopping through the woods, with a fox coming his way, mouth open. Still he smiles and never alters his pace. The Sheriff did not want the enemy to know they had him worried. He wanted to keep them guessing. With his arms folded across his chest, he stared out of the window. In his mind, Sheriff Champ kept constructing the various possible scenarios and none ended peacefully. Shimmering stars illuminated the moonless, jet black sky, as if to remind him that even in darkness there is still light. A cold sweat glistened on his furrowed brow as he nervously paced the floor. In the night's silence, the wall clock was ticking like a time bomb. Sheriff Champ filled the kettle to make coffee as his eyes kept darting toward the telephone that refused to ring. Dread of what he knew was possible had his stomach locked up tight. That dread was like an invisible demon sitting heavy on his shoulders; He could almost hear the sharpening of its knives. As the night dwindled away the tension in Sheriff Champ grew.

Tulsa's Black Wall Street

A story of Greenwood Oklahoma

Facing the inevitable, he knew there was no other option but to warn the Mayor of his fears; either way he had to know.

On the morning of May 30th 1921, Sheriff Champ slowly rose from bed after a restless night. His mind offered only one thought; "Today is the day." There was no avoiding it. His gut told him something bad was coming and he could no more stop what was coming than he could call upon the clouds to clear the sky. With his head spinning, he carefully dialed the Mayor's telephone number. Sheriff Champ desperately tried to control the tremor in his voice to disguise how fearful he was. The Sheriff warned Mayor Elliott that trouble was brewing. He was almost prophetic in meticulously explaining what was on the horizon and desperately implored the Mayor to do something. Hardly a gifted leader, the Mayor was uneasy about getting involved. He ended the telephone call, citing a previous appointment. The appointment he referenced was playing golf with local citizens. The dread of what he suspected would happen, now crept over him like an icy chill; numbing his brain. That day all the food he placed in his mouth tasted like cardboard. No amount of chewing made it possible to swallow. He was jumpy and his nerves were frayed to the quick.

Tulsa's Black Wall Street
A story of Greenwood Oklahoma

In his building anxiety he tried to construct elaborate rationalizations for why everything would turn out alright, but still the nagging voice in the back of his mind spoke of nothing but doom ahead. Each tick of the clock dragged him helpless and nervous to the unknown allotted time.

Tulsa's Black Wall Street

A story of Greenwood Oklahoma

Chapter 13

Having exhausted every other avenue, the Sheriff made one desperate final appeal to the black churches. In describing what he believed was an impending calamitous situation where there would be no winners he earnestly asked the church to mediate. Agreeing to assist an emergency community meeting was called. In that community meeting, the clergy pleaded for calm, forgiveness and understanding. Additionally, they were requesting patience, indicating Tulsa was seeking change and change took time. But blacks, especially younger ones, were fed up. One young man summed it up succinctly in responding, "I did not start out angry, I started out as a man who simply wanted to be treated equally. I am sick and tired of the 'it takes time' justification. All of his life, white people told my father 'it takes time'. All of my grandfather's life, he was told 'it takes time'. All of my great-grandfather's life he was also told 'it takes time'. No disrespect Reverend, but the time is up. I'm tired of being angry, sad and afraid. We can double down on our efforts to be victorious in battle or sit back and be prey. It is our choice and our path whether we will be the sheep or the wolf.

Tulsa's Black Wall Street
A story of Greenwood Oklahoma

If Tulsa doesn't come around, we're gonna burn it down." Blacks had witnessed their rising hopes for full acceptance citizenship turn into terrifying disappointments. Instead of equal opportunity they received segregation and white supremacist terrorism in the forms of lynching, rape and murder.

It was the morning of May 30th 1921. Easy awoke before dawn into a blackness of fear and concern. Anticipating that trouble was inevitable, he could feel the walls of violence closing in around him. Similar to Sheriff Champ, Easy was troubled by what he believed to be bad times coming. Willie stepped from the back and stared at Easy for a while with a raised eyebrow. Easy was sitting tense on the couch, with his back arched and his eyes focused on the front door. "Easy, are you okay?" Willie asked. "Yeah, fine," Easy mumbled, his eyes shifting nervously. Willie could see that Easy was troubled and in deep thought. Shaking him slightly, Willie said "Hey, Easy look at me man."

Willie took off his sun shades and steps back to get a good look at Easy. He could see it in Easy's eyes, something was troubling him. "What's wrong brother?" Willie asked with genuine concern.

Tulsa's Black Wall Street
A story of Greenwood Oklahoma

Easy got up on his feet and told Willie that everything had gone wrong. Things were in a terrible mess and there was no good way out. He told Willie that he had been keeping a secret from the world and that secret was like an acid eating at his guts. Easy confided to Willie about his ongoing relationship with Emma and that he had to urgently get word to her. However every white person in Tulsa would be constantly looking at every move of a black face. Despite the close scrutiny and risk, Easy just had to get word to Emma. A heavy silence settled over them, thicker than the uneasy tension in the atmosphere. After the initial shock dissipated Willie placed his hand on Easy's shoulder. He said, "Man, I told you once that you were the only living person that I genuinely trusted. As long as there is a breath in my body, no matter the trouble whether you are at fault or not, I will have your back. Big or small, I am your nigger. Thick or thin, I am all in." Then with that slick Willie smirk, he asked, "What can I do to help you?" Danger had always been like an aphrodisiac to Willie. He loved the thrill and excitement of endangerment. The more extreme the peril the better he liked it. Willie took to trouble, like a pig to mud. Easy found Willie's support reassuring, not only what he said, but more by the way he said it.

Tulsa's Black Wall Street
A story of Greenwood Oklahoma

Easy was going into Tulsa and asked that Willie wait for him at the business until he returned.

Easy made his way to Tulsa's Drexel building, where Emma was on duty. Mindful of his surroundings, he carefully watched until her elevator was vacant. Cautiously, he entered the elevator asking Emma for a ride to the top floor. Emma's was the only elevator in the building and the top-floor restroom was restricted to blacks. He explained the precarious nature of events indicating they would have to avoid seeing each other until things calmed down. Obviously concerned he begged that she be attentive and careful to avoid potential danger. Employing their secret codes they would correspond only by mail using their private pen names. Distracted in conversation, Emma did not stop the elevator exactly flush with the floor.

Stepping from the elevator, Easy stumbled. In Emma's concern she tried to keep him from falling and momentarily lost her balance. Fearing that she would fall, Emma squealed. Easy immediately knew that a black man anywhere within eyeshot of a white woman squealing added up to big trouble. To avoid any misunderstanding or trying to explain, Easy quickly rushed off.

Tulsa's Black Wall Street
A story of Greenwood Oklahoma

A clerk at Renberg's, a clothing store that was located on the first floor of the Drexel, heard what he thought sounded like a woman's scream. Looking out he saw a black man rushing from the building. The clerk went to the elevator and found Emma in what he described as "a distraught state." Despite her protests that she was fine, he believed she had been assaulted and summoned authorities.

Minutes later Sheriff Champ arrived at the Drexel building. After taking a statement, the clerk pointed Emma out to the Sheriff. As he slowly walked toward Emma the Sheriff removed his hat and extended a courteous greeting in a husky drawl. Showing genuine concern for Emma, the Sheriff attempted to convey empathetic words to determine what had happened in the elevator. Identifying Easy as the man in the elevator, Emma tried to describe in detail what happened to clear the matter. She related to the Sheriff that she had known Easy since childhood and he was a decent man. Easy only used the elevator to gain access to the top floor where there was a colored restroom. On the way back down she failed to stop the elevator exactly flush with the floor. As he stepped off he tripped. In an effort to assist him from falling she lost her balance and stupidly she squealed. Continuing she said, "That was all there was to it.

Tulsa's Black Wall Street

A story of Greenwood Oklahoma

Did someone think something happened?" Sheriff Champ explained that someone reported what was believed to be an incident and he was merely following up. The Sheriff informed Emma that he wanted to keep the investigation low-key to avoid the episode being blown out of proportion. Emma reiterated that nothing happened, Easy was incapable of such a thing and there was no need to investigate further or press charges. Sheriff Champ agreed with Emma.

Regardless of whether or not assault had occurred, Easy had plenty reason to be fearful. Just the rumor of such an accusation alone, even false, placed his life in jeopardy. Truth can only be seen by those with truth in them. Gossip and lies are nasty diseases and the Ku Klux Klan was infected. When the Klan had difficulty peddling hate, they told lies. Rumors of what had happened at the Drexel building started almost immediately. The rumors were flying thick and spreading like a wild fire. Assumptions quickly turned to the sexual. The details of what transpired varied from person to person, but accounts of the incident circulated among the city's white community throughout the day and became more exaggerated with each telling.

Tulsa's Black Wall Street

A story of Greenwood Oklahoma

By night, rumor had it that four or five black bucks from Greenwood and on drugs had attacked a white girl. Not only did they rape her, but they also cut her up. Rumors had it that they cut her on the legs, arms, face and even cut off one of her breasts as a trophy. Easy was supposedly leading the attack. The mere fact that none of this was true did not hinder the Klan from spreading these lies nor did it deter whites from believing it. These rumors had also spread to a militant and antagonistic black community that knew the rumors were false. The general consensus was that the community would be vigilant and forcefully defend themselves if a black person was endangered. Based on the rumors circling through Tulsa, four or five black men had brutally attacked a white woman. Greenwood residents rightfully reckoned that white justice mandated an aggressive action, namely a lynching. They were having none of it. They reasoned the only time a man with a gun would pause, was when he was facing a gun. Blacks may die, but whites would be going to the cemetery also.

Troubled, Sheriff Champ was in his office late into the night. Despite doing everything right, rage was building like deep water currents. The whole situation was a God damn mess and there was no way he could stop it, reverse it or slow it down.

Tulsa's Black Wall Street
A story of Greenwood Oklahoma

He suspected that most of city officials, including the Mayor, had been corrupted. The Sheriff had no idea who he could turn to or who he could to trust. As an honorable man, the Sheriff had been waiting for, praying for, some kind of top-down change of mindset within city government. He had hoped to see an improvement in race relations. However, he all but knew now that he was fooling himself if he thought things would change for the better. The Sheriff was on the edge, as a God fearing man, he had a sense of obligation to no longer turn a blind eye. He saw death as being much too late to beg God for absolution. The Sheriff saw this mess as a test from God and an opportunity to save his soul.

Doing the right thing usually costs rather than pays, but doing the right thing brings health to the soul. Of all the things in life that hold a lasting significance, it is those right things that always shine bright. Sheriff Champ was certainly no saint or hero either, but he was God fearing and did have a sense of integrity. Perhaps he had not gotten it completely right in the past, but he still had time to do the right thing.

Tulsa's Black Wall Street
A story of Greenwood Oklahoma

Chapter 14

The following day was Tuesday, May 31, 1921. The very first thing Sheriff Champ did that morning was direct the city's two black officers to detain Easy. With the tension levels where they were, the last thing Sheriff Champ wanted was an overzealous white officer to make a tenuous situation worse. Instead, he was making every effort to calm the storm. On a personal note the Sheriff told the officers that he strongly believed trouble was on the horizon. He explained that, "I wish that I could go into a time machine right now and stop all of this. But wishing won't do it. If I wished in one hand and crapped in the other, we all know which hand would fill the fastest. When something bad happens we all have three choices. We can let it define you, let it destroy you, or you can let it strengthen you. Gentlemen I sincerely hope this strengthens us all." He made it perfectly clear to the officers that Easy was not a suspect. The Sheriff needed an official statement from Easy to finish his police report. As the officers departed, the Sheriff reminded them, "remember stay calm and keep everything calm."

Tulsa's Black Wall Street
A story of Greenwood Oklahoma

The two officers located Easy on Greenwood Avenue at his business where he and Willie sat drinking coffee. The officers calmly explained the reason for their visit and requested Easy accompany them to the Tulsa jail to speak with the Sheriff. Word of Easy being detained quickly spread throughout both Greenwood and Tulsa.

As the two men met and sat to talk Easy found the Sheriff to be friendly and sociable. In a relaxed manner he told Easy, "I will be honest with you or else hold my tongue. I need to finish my report and you don't have to fear a hidden agenda. I need your recollection of events two days ago at the Drexel building. All I ask is that you be truthful. Identical to Emma's story, he related that she had known Emma and her brother Joseph since childhood. He asked Emma to visit the top floor to use the colored restroom. On the way back down she failed to stop the elevator exactly flush with the floor. As he stepped off he tripped. In an effort to keep him from falling she lost her balance and squealed as she fell. He then looked at the Sheriff and said, "I was not about to hang around after she squealed. The fact that I am here now justifies me not sticking around."

Tulsa's Black Wall Street

A story of Greenwood Oklahoma

The Sheriff listened intently to Easy talk. His eyes, probed Easy's body language desperately wanting to get a feel for his truthfulness. He finally cleared his throat and told Easy, "I know something's not right; and I don't believe that story." Stunned, Easy asked "what do you mean you don't believe my story?" The Sheriff stood, walked over and closed his office door. Returning to his seat, he told Easy, "I know that you did not assault that young woman. You both were truthful about that. I don't believe for a second you were on that elevator just to go to the restroom. But for the sake of my report, it is closed. I think the clerk at Renberg's clothing store made a mountain out of a mole hill." The Sheriff closed his file folder and told Easy, "Respect is more than passing pleasantries, more than nice words. It takes effort to look at someone of another race and take in who they are, to show them you regard their point of view with compassion and seriousness. It is listening without judgement, getting to know them with as few assumptions as possible. It is in careful understanding conveyed by empathic words and deeds to show the depth of feeling you hold for them. In this way respect is foundational for trust. I hope that we can build a mutual respect."

Tulsa's Black Wall Street
A story of Greenwood Oklahoma

In the middle of their conversation one of his officers knocked on the office door interrupting Easy and Sheriff Champ. Shaking his head, an officer entered and hands Sheriff Champ a copy of the evening edition of the Tulsa Tribune newspaper. The Tribune was one of two white-owned papers in Tulsa and it printed the story of Easy's arrest. The afternoon's edition headline read: Negro Nabbed for Attacking Girl in Elevator and described the alleged assault. The word rape was rarely used in newspapers during the early 20th century. Instead, assault was used to describe such an attack. Their fabricated account ripe with innuendo, however it was thin on facts. The same edition included an editorial warning of a potential lynching of the alleged attacker entitled: Lynch a Negro Tonight. The editorial maintained that Negroes were becoming too impertinent and out of their place to openly assault a white woman. After first slamming the paper onto his desk, the Sheriff asked rhetorically, "How in the hell did they know all of this?" Easy learned how to read people early on. He was a very analytical person, paying close attention to Sheriff Champ in understanding the severity of this situation.

Tulsa's Black Wall Street

A story of Greenwood Oklahoma

Easy was sensitive to the fact that he had a personal interest in how developing circumstances would emerge. A muscle twitched involuntarily at the corner of the Sheriff's right eye and his mouth formed a rigid grimace. With arms folded tightly across his chest he tapped his foot furiously while staring out of the office window. He paced up and down as if determined to wear a hole in the floor.

Easy finally spoke up to puncture the near silence. He said to the Sheriff, "I can see that you are genuinely stressed and trapped in your head. I believe that you're trying to do the right thing and I respect you for that. But I must tell you, despite your best efforts you are being undermined and doomed to fail. For my own benefit, I can put this mess into perspective if you care to listen." Sheriff Champ realized that everything hinged on what he did and did not do that day. Puzzled, he asked Easy, "What makes you so certain that you know what I am not aware of?" Without flinching, Easy responded "Because I have an inside source." Initially, the Sheriff was idly curious, but now Easy had his undivided attention. "What do you want from me?' Sheriff Champ asked. Before providing Sheriff Champ insight, he requested that the Sheriff, keep Deputy Letchworth completely in the dark about their conversation.

Tulsa's Black Wall Street
A story of Greenwood Oklahoma

He then asked the Sheriff to inform Kenneth Chase Jr. of his location and tell him privately that "Easy needs to see him." Easy told the Sheriff that Jr. would substantiate everything he would tell the Sheriff. Taken aback that Easy would call Kenneth Chase Jr., son of the Grand Wizard, to substantiate a story the Sheriff moved with no delay. He immediately called down and ordered Deputy Letchworth to monitor the city limits for disturbances. To allow for discretion he dispatched a second officer to bring Kenneth Chase Jr. to the Courthouse or have him to call for the Sheriff.

They left the jail discreetly relocating to the courthouse. Easy and Sheriff Champ sat in the courthouse judge's chamber waiting for Jr. to show. Word of the Tulsa Tribune story had spread like wildfire. Shortly after the Tulsa Tribune hit the streets, word of the arrest inundated conversations in both the white and black communities. Each new rumor was like gas being tossed on the burning fire of rage. An uncontrollable anger began building through the communities demanding release in the form of violence. This was the break the Klan had been looking for.

Tulsa's Black Wall Street

A story of Greenwood Oklahoma

They had been desperate for any excuse to "run the niggers out of Tulsa and take their property and land." However black residents were not having any of it. They refused to stand idly by as whites tried to lynch another innocent Black man. Willie had heard enough saying, "You can sit on your asses selling wolf tickets but I want brother Easy to know I got his back. This is our call to arms my friends. We can either be the hammer or the nail."

After about ninety minutes, Kenneth Jr. arrived. He decided to drive himself over after speaking with the police office. Knowing his father was a cautious man, he did not want to accompany the office and arouse his father's suspicion. Bearing a strong resemblance to father, Jr. was a younger version of Kenneth Sr. Surveying his surroundings, Jr. walked into the judge's chambers like the floor would give in. Every step was so light that he barely made a sound. It was visible from his facial expression and body language that he was nervous. He seemed almost relieved as he spotted Easy. Greeting Jr. Easy asked, "You okay?" His mouth was almost too dry to speak, but he nodded and said "Yeah, Easy, I'm okay." Easy explained to Jr. "I wanted to enlighten the Sheriff about problems within his office. I asked him to invite you here to substantiate what I tell him. Will you do that for me?"

Tulsa's Black Wall Street
A story of Greenwood Oklahoma

Jr. agreed. Easy went on to tell the Sheriff that he and Jr. had been friends since childhood, along with Emma and her brother. The clerk who reported the assault was a Klan member and friend to Kenneth Sr. The clerk has joked around town about embellishing the story. Deputy Letchworth was not only in the Klan, but was Kenneth Sr.'s trusted enforcer. Deputy Letchworth has been leaking information from the Sheriff's office since his arrival. In fact Deputy Letchworth was the unknown mob member that knocked you unconscious during the lynching of Walter Oakley." Kenneth Jr. interrupted Easy to tell the Sheriff, "What Easy has told you is true, I know because I told him everything. Easy is a friend that I owe my life. Deputy Letchworth also conspired with my father in the lynching of Isaac Washington. They planned and carried out the bombing of those three churches to distract you and allow the Deputy to gain custody of Isaac. Once you were out of the picture, my father knew poor Isaac had no hope. The sad truth is the savage beating my sister received from the alleged assault was actually received from my father; not an attacker. The only thing Isaac was guilty of was being a Negro.

Tulsa's Black Wall Street
A story of Greenwood Oklahoma

Deputy Letchworth also told my father about you detaining Easy. My father called the newspapers and provided details and his version of the assault. He wanted to rile every civic minded white citizen for support to justify a lynching. But, I owe Easy, so I had to tell you the truth. Sheriff you have a cancer in your office. My father is ruthless and sees himself as a protector of the white race. He will stop at nothing short of the complete annihilation of anything that is not white. Unfortunately he and I no longer see eye to eye." There was seriousness in Kenneth Jr. and his words unnerved Sheriff Champ.

While still gathering additional facts from Kenneth Jr. the Sheriff heard a commotion outside the courthouse. He stepped from the backroom and glanced outside the side window. Observing a large crowd of whites congregating in front of the jail he thought, "Well so much for discretion." The town apparently already knew where they were located. About that time one of the deputies securing the courthouse informed the Sheriff that an anonymous caller had telephoned the jail and threatened Easy's life. The Sheriff thanked Kenneth Jr. for his invaluable insight and assured him that Easy would get out of town okay. He told Kenneth Jr. "Thanks to you Easy will safe and be out of here before midnight; I promise.

Tulsa's Black Wall Street
A story of Greenwood Oklahoma

They won't anticipate me using their hate and predictability as a weapon against them." The Sheriff urged Kenneth Jr. to quickly exit out the back. Before departing, he and Easy exchanged a few words in private. Surprising, they both even shared a laugh.

It was slightly past 7 p.m. white people continued their muster outside the courthouse. Biding time, the Sheriff placed his men on full alert. Intent on averting the breakdown that led to Isaac Washington being lynched the Sheriff organized his officers into a defensive formation around the courthouse. Easy was moved from the Judge's chambers to a room behind the balcony on the second floor. The Sheriff next positioned his officers, armed with rifles and shotguns, on the roof of the courthouse. He locked and barricaded all law enforcement inside the courthouse. All officers were given orders to shoot intruders on sight. The Sheriff then went outside and tried to talk the crowd into going home to no avail. Seething with anger the mob hooted the Sheriff down. Three white men approached Sheriff Champ from the crowd. For the sanctity of "white womanhood" the men demanded that the "guilty nigger" be turned over to them. Despite being out numbered, the Sheriff was successful in turning the men away.

Tulsa's Black Wall Street
A story of Greenwood Oklahoma

Chapter 15

A few blocks away on Greenwood Avenue, members of the black community were gathering to discuss the situation at the courthouse. Given the recent lynching of Isaac Washington, they had little doubt that Easy was at great risk. The community was determined to prevent the lynching of another black man, but divided about the tactics to be used. Young World War I veterans were preparing for a battle by collecting guns and ammunition. Older, more prosperous men feared a destructive confrontation that likely would cost them dearly. Hezekiah White and O. W. Gurley walked to the courthouse, unarmed, where the sheriff assured them that there would be no lynching. Although greatly concerned for his son's safety, Easy asked his father to trust in the Sheriff. Returning to Greenwood, Hezekiah and Gurley tried to calm the group, but failed. Around 7:30 pm, a mob of approximately 30 black men, armed with rifles and shotguns, decided to go to the courthouse and support the sheriff and his deputies to defend Easy from the mob.

Tulsa's Black Wall Street
A story of Greenwood Oklahoma

Assuring them that Easy was safe, the Sheriff allowed Easy to speak with Willie privately. Willie encouraged the men to return home.

Having seen the brazenness of blacks arming themselves infuriated Kenneth Sr. Seeing blacks being permitted to approach the courthouse dictated that whites take control. In retaliation for the perceived disrespect, the mob headed for the National Guard armory where they planned to arm themselves. The armory contained a supply of small arms and ammunition. Major John Smith of the 29th Infantry had already learned of the mounting situation downtown and the possibility of a break-in. He was pro-active and had taken appropriate measures to prevent disorder. Major Smith called the commanders of the other National Guard units in Tulsa. Guard members were ordered to put on their uniforms and report immediately to the armory. When the mob of white men arrived and began pulling at the window grating over a window, Major Smith went outside to confront them. Major Smith informed them the Guard members inside were armed and prepared to shoot anyone who tried to enter. After the Major's show of force, the mob withdrew from the armory.

Tulsa's Black Wall Street
A story of Greenwood Oklahoma

With the mob temporarily away, for approximately two hours, the courthouse was quiet. Now night time, the outside was etched in charcoal providing cover for Sheriff Champ's plan. Blending into the night's shadows, the Sheriff secretly smuggled Easy from the courthouse disguised as a police officer. The mob's unforeseen departure allowed the Sheriff to make his move sooner than planned. This was a good thing that Easy was freed, but he had prearranged to meet Willie approximately two hours later. Because he obviously could not wait around, Easy decided to let his parents know he was safe. Taking side streets protected by darkness, Easy made his way to his parents' home. Easy informed his father of plans to leave town giving the situation time to cool down, but asked that he get word to Willie. He told his father that he would wait for Willie down by Worley's creek.

White people from the mob returned to the courthouse in mass. Many returned home to gather and stock-up on additional weapons. Anxiety on Greenwood Avenue was also rising. Unaware that he had been smuggled out of the courthouse, the black community was worried about Easy's safety.

Tulsa's Black Wall Street
A story of Greenwood Oklahoma

Small groups of armed black men began to venture toward the courthouse in automobiles, partly for reconnaissance, and to demonstrate they were prepared to take necessary action to protect Easy. In Greenwood, rumors began to fly. One report that whites were storming the courthouse created an overwhelming anxiety. Fear engulfed Willie, knocking all other thoughts aside. Sometime after 10 pm, a second, larger mob of black men returned to the courthouse. Once again, they offered their support to the sheriff, who again declined their help. He assured them that Easy was in no danger and there was nothing to worry about. The Sheriff asked that they return to their homes. The black presence sparked a great deal of shouting, harsh words and insults between the whites and blacks. A white man, in the crowd, seeing Willie's shotgun shouted, "Yea nigger. Be a good boy and go home. By the way, what do you plan to do with that shotgun?" "I had planned to use it," Willie calmly responded. "Hell no nigger, you will not use it. Give me that shotgun now," the white man demanded. The white man did not know it, but there was nothing worse than trying to face down Willie Weathers.

Tulsa's Black Wall Street

A story of Greenwood Oklahoma

In the case of confrontation or a perceived threat Willie lost all rationality and became a monster that would do anything. He was similar to dynamite in that he was either safely boxed in a crate or exploding. Now smiling, Willie handed the shotgun to the white man then said, "Yes sir. You can have the shotgun. You are right I will not use it." But Willie then pulled a pistol the man had not seen and said, "But I will use this one you peckerwood." Willie then pointed the pistol directly to the man's head and blew his brains out. The gunshot triggered an almost immediate response by the white men. They began firing on the blacks, who continued firing back at the whites. The exchange of gunfire only lasted a few seconds, but it exacted an enormous toll. Ten whites and two blacks lay dead or dying in the street. The black contingent retreated toward Greenwood as a rolling gunfight ensued. The armed white mob pursued the black group toward Greenwood with both sides stopping to loot local stores for additional weapons and ammunition. Along the way innocent bystanders were killed. Twelve people were killed leaving a movie theater as they were caught off guard by the mob. The white mob began firing indiscriminately at any black in the crowd, accidently killing one of their own men in the confusion.

Tulsa's Black Wall Street
A story of Greenwood Oklahoma

Overwhelmed by the sheer number of whites, and their greater firepower, blacks retreated to Greenwood Avenue into their own part of town and took up a defensive position behind the Frisco train depot. Whites set up positions and a machine gun emplacement on the top of a nearby hill. A train came through Tulsa's Frisco station around midnight. Caught between two hostile factions, the train took on significant gunfire from both sides of the tracks. Passengers in the train were lying flat on the floor as a regular volley of bullets rained through the train's windows.

Stunned by a perceived "negro uprising", the Mayor reached out to Major Smith at the National Guard Armory for emergency support. Major Smith placed an immediate call and conveyed the Mayor's concerns to the Oklahoma National Guard Adjutant General in Oklahoma City. In keeping his chain of command abreast of the disturbance, the Adjutant General communicated to the Governor. The Governor was the only person who could mobilize the unit, and he could not officially do so unless the civil authorities felt that they were no longer able to control the situation. The Governor approved mobilizing the National Guard.

Tulsa's Black Wall Street

A story of Greenwood Oklahoma

Unit officers were directed to only guard the armory, and they were only to assist the civil authorities if necessary. Around midnight Tulsa Oklahoma's National Guard unit began to assemble at the armory. They were organized and provided a plan to subdue the mob and bring the town back to order. Groups of sentries were deployed to guard the courthouse, police station and other public facilities. Members of the local American Legion joined in on patrols of the streets. From the viewpoint of black residents, the forces appeared to have been deployed to protect only the white districts. This manner of deployment and perceived slight to them did not sit well with the black community. An added irritant making the circumstance worse was that the National Guard began rounding up blacks who had not returned to Greenwood.

After retreating from Tulsa, Willie headed to Hezekiah's place. The area was not safe and he was cautious in his surroundings to avoid making a sound. In a flash of shock and dread Willie began hyper-ventilating thinking Easy might not be left to his own devices. He was supposed to be waiting for Easy around midnight but there was too much heat for Willie in town after killing that redneck. All Willie could do was pray that Hezekiah was home.

Tulsa's Black Wall Street
A story of Greenwood Oklahoma

He dreaded having to give Hezekiah such bad news, but there was still time. If Hezekiah was home he could easily make it there to pick up Easy. Finally Willie made it to Hezekiah's home the moment that he had been dreading had arrived. Happiness is what Willie felt when Hezekiah opened the door. Before he could say a word, Hezekiah told Willie that he had just missed Easy. Willie's eyes and mouth were frozen wide open in an expression of stunned surprise. Although he was staring straight at Hezekiah, Willie was rendered speechless scrambling to make sense of it all. Hezekiah explained how Easy had been smuggled out of the courthouse earlier than planned. He also gave Willie the message that Easy would be waiting by Worley's creek. Hezekiah took Willie to where Easy was hiding out.

After initially worrying that he had let his friend down, Willie breathed easier. His heart beat a little faster at seeing a friend that he loved as a brother. They embraced at finding one another safe and sound. But the manner in which whites and the justice system had treated him provoked a deep seated anger in Easy. He had been lied about, falsely accused, detained and had his life threatened. The entire episode had been skillfully and carefully manipulated by white racists.

Tulsa's Black Wall Street

A story of Greenwood Oklahoma

The chief architect was the Ku Klux Klan and thanks to Jr., Easy knew the entire story. Kenneth Sr. was the Klan's ring leader and Easy would bare a grudge against him until he died or took revenge, whichever came first. His need for revenge was like a rat gnawing at his soul. He wanted revenge for all the mistreatment, terror, assaults, murders and lynching's. Easy had a desperate need for Kenneth Sr. to know and suffer the same anguish. Easy's need for revenge thrilled Willie and appealed to his twisted dark side. Willie told Easy, "When a man is denied the basic right to live like a man, he has no other choice but to take matters into his own hands. Easy, this is what I do best. We got this." While still in custody, Easy laid some groundwork for his plan of revenge with Kenneth Jr. At some point the mob would finally discover Easy was no longer in custody and Kenneth Sr. would be livid. Kenneth Jr. would provide a hint and drive Kenneth Sr. to Worley's creek. In hatching their scheme Willie and Easy planned every minute detail; even a contingency plan. Giving them a taste of their own medicine Easy decided to employ the Klan's own strategy of misdirection to assure they discover that Easy was gone. The only thing remaining was to wait the next few hours until 5 a.m.

Tulsa's Black Wall Street
A story of Greenwood Oklahoma

Chapter 16

At around 1 am, the white mob began setting fires, mainly in businesses on the southern edge of the Greenwood district. As crews from the Tulsa Fire Department arrived to put out the fires, they were turned away at gunpoint. By 4 am, an estimated two-dozen black-owned businesses had been set ablaze. As news traveled among Greenwood residents in the early morning hours, many began to take up arms in defense of their community, while others began a mass exodus from the city. Throughout the day and into the night both sides continued fighting.

Around 5 a.m. whites heard multiple explosions coming from Tulsa. The Mayor's home, an oil executive's home and one of Tulsa's banks were firebombed. The fire siren's wail broke through the noise of gunfire and the mob thought it was a train whistle. Whites mistakenly feared the whistle was a signal for blacks to launch an attack and the explosions were an all-out assault on the Tulsa courthouse. Splitting into two groups, part of the mob made their way back to the courthouse and the remaining mob poured into Greenwood.

Tulsa's Black Wall Street

A story of Greenwood Oklahoma

Crowds of white people poured into Greenwood both on foot and by vehicle. Five white men in a car led the charge, but were killed by a hail of gunfire before they had traveled a block. Afterward chaos ensued as the white mob began shooting indiscriminately killing old, young, woman and children on their rampage. The mob broke into houses and buildings, looting. During the chaos one white looter was overheard saying, "This nigger has a piano. I worked here all my life and I ain't got a piano. How does that look a nigger got what I aint?" The angry looter then ordered the unarmed family onto the streets before setting the house ablaze. Once on the streets, some blacks were shot. Fortunate black residents were able to make it to the National Guard's detention center. At the time of the riot, Dr. A.C. Jackson, considered the "most able negro surgeon in America" was shot to death as he left his house. When rumors had it that one black church was being used as a fortress and armory the riffraff firebombed the building shooting into the crowd as they ran for their lives. A 92 year old black woman, who struggled to aid her deaf husband to safety was much too slow and was shot three times.

Tulsa's Black Wall Street
A story of Greenwood Oklahoma

The mob placed a rope around the old man's neck and dragged him through the Greenwood business district behind a car. Many were believed to have died when trapped by the flames. In their "take no prisoner" strategy white people even dispatched several planes from the nearby Curtiss-Southwest Field outside Tulsa. White assailants were witnessed to have fired rifles and dropped firebombs from airplanes onto buildings, homes, and fleeing families. The satisfaction of security was now nothing but a distant memory for these black residents. An invisible force of anxiety seemed to crush them from every possible direction.

After encountering a number of black refugees, National Guard troop began to take them in custody. Troops collect all the inhabitants they can and offer protection by marching them to the convention center. The breakneck pace at which the violence was escalating was taking a toll on the National Guard. Engaging in so many activities spread their limited manpower thin and adequate support proved to be unsustainable. The strain of trying to maintain order, protect government assets, provide medical assistance, aid fire and rescue took its toll. The second mob group broke into the courthouse only to find Easy gone.

Tulsa's Black Wall Street

A story of Greenwood Oklahoma

Bloodthirsty, Kenneth Sr. was determined to find Easy at all costs. He erupted like a volcano. With a burning rage he screamed, "Brothers, we are going to find this nigger if its takes all year and we are going to make this city safe for our white women. There isn't a place that nigger can hide, that we can't find him. Find him and destroy him we will. I don't much care how it happens I just need him to suffer. I just need his black eyes extinguished from this universe. And boys, there are no rules." As he hissed his poisonous rhetoric he demanded loyalty from the mob in enforcing his violence. The mob had now become mindless in following Kenneth Sr.'s every lead. There were cheers and battle calls from the mob rising in volume like thunder. Today they were going to take their stand and fight. At Kenneth Sr.'s orders the mob went to the homes of many affluent white families who employed blacks as live-in cooks, domestics and servants. Leaving no stone unturned, they demanded that white families turn over their employees. Kenneth Sr. did not want one black person in Tulsa. After removing all black employees from Tulsa, there would be no legitimate reason for them to be there.

Tulsa's Black Wall Street
A story of Greenwood Oklahoma

Any black spotted past this day would be shot on sight. Many white families complied, however those who refused were subjected to attacks and vandalism.

On June 1, 1921 The Oklahoma National Guard's Adjutant General arrived from Oklahoma City by special train at approximately 9:30 a.m. with additional troops. After witnessing the carnage and hysteria first hand, the Adjutant General immediately summoned reinforcements. The local National Guard unit had a limited number of members. They might be able to battle an army of blacks at their defensive front, but the troops were no match for the two thousand or so heavily armed white men. By the time of his arrival most of the surviving black citizens had either fled the city or were in custody at the various detention centers. The primary goal and first direction from the Adjutant General was to disarm the armed white citizens.

Nobody in Tulsa liked the Adjutant General much, yet no one really disliked him. He possessed an intolerant manner, was a bit forward, a little intrusive, but it was clear that his no-nonsense approach was effective. Within two hours of him imposing his will, the situation quickly improved.

Tulsa's Black Wall Street

A story of Greenwood Oklahoma

By 11 a.m. firing began to diminish. Most of Greenwood residences were empty, except for a few Blacks who were being ousted in a house to house search. The Governor declared Martial law at 11:49 am and by noon the National Guard had managed to suppress most of the remaining violence. Guardsmen assisted firemen in putting out fires and took imprisoned blacks out of the hands of vigilantes. As directed, the National Guard imprisoned all blacks (men, women and children) not already interned. As many as 6,000 blacks were held under armed guard detention at the Convention Hall, Baseball Park and Fairgrounds.

Approximately twenty-four hours after the violence erupted, it had all but ceased. When the dust finally settled, over a thousand buildings, mostly in the Greenwood District, were destroyed. Homes, businesses, and churches that were thriving the week before were suddenly nothing but rubble. In the wake of the violence 35 city blocks lay in charred ruins, an estimated 10,000 people were left homeless and hundreds were killed. The exact number of blacks killed was unknown, but the state hired forty seven gravediggers.

Tulsa's Black Wall Street
A story of Greenwood Oklahoma

There was a rush to bury bodies and no official records were maintained of those many burials.

Kenneth Sr.'s rants and tantrums were legendary. However restraints placed on Tulsa by a no-nonsense Adjutant General had him acting like a well-mannered child in Sunday school. He may have lost his ability to publicly lash out, but he had lost none of his contempt for black people nor had he forgotten his promise to find Easy. Leaving Tulsa, Kenneth Sr. was frothing at the mouth and determined to make an example of Easy. Later that same afternoon, just outside of Tulsa, Kenneth Sr. was alone skulking around Worley's creek. From behind Kenneth Sr. hears someone ask, "Looking for someone?" Turning slowly, he sees Easy standing behind him holding a shotgun. Sneering, Kenneth Sr. said, "My hat is off to you boy. I must admit that you are one slippery nigger. But you ain't as smart as you think you are." Easy wanted to run up and beat the living daylights out of him, but he remained cool. "I am smart enough to know that you would be here. I am smart enough to have the drop on you and I am smart enough to know that I can't let you live. I am about to send you straight to hell, where you belong." Kenneth Sr. let out an understated sigh and turned to walk away, showing he wasn't afraid to turn his back.

Tulsa's Black Wall Street

A story of Greenwood Oklahoma

Easy pulled back the triggers on the shotgun, "If you take one more step I will cut you down like the dog you are." Almost being dismissive, Kenneth Sr. told Easy "Hell, you don't frighten me boy. Now follow me to my truck; that is if you ain't a scared nigger. I want you to understand me and I have something I want you to see."

Easy, always trusted his gut instincts and when he felt something was wrong, it usually was. Understanding the existing climate in Tulsa, Easy knew the closer attention he paid to his surroundings the safer he was going to be. They were operating in an environment where there was a great deal of uncertainty and risk. In such an environment, even a tiny mistake was a matter of life and death. Easy was a bit curious about what Kenneth Sr. was up to and decided to briefly play along. The truck was on open ground and only a brief distant, so keeping an eye on his every movement was not a difficult undertaking. After reaching the truck, Kenneth Sr. stopped, turned and damn-it if he wasn't smirking at Easy. He then pointed to a bloodied quilt that was covering something on the back of his truck.

Tulsa's Black Wall Street
A story of Greenwood Oklahoma

Arrogantly, Kenneth Sr. told Easy, "The only people who say that I'm callous are the bleeding hearts and weak kneed, do-gooder losers that just don't cut it. Those dumbasses need to learn that it is a dog eat dog world and the winner takes all." As if he had left his emotions at home there was a look of triumph in his eyes when he pulled back the bloodied quilt on the back of that rust bucket of a truck. Easy looked in horror and disbelief at what he saw. Under the blanket was the crumpled and badly battered body of Kenneth Jr.; dead. The old man bellowed in anger, "That boy was nothing but a weak and pathetic loser. He had no balls whatsoever." Now blinded by a five-course serving of rage Kenneth Sr. told Easy that he knew Jr. had spilled his guts to the Sheriff, telling him everything. He could almost forgive Jr. for that, but spilling his guts to a Nigger was unforgivable. He admitted torturing and killing his son however, in an odd reasoning he blamed Easy saying "I curse you for saving him from drowning years ago." Then Kenneth Sr. admitted, "Kenneth Jr. did not want to talk, but I beat the truth out of him. The damn fool actually thought I would spare his life. I know you wanted to trap me here alone so I decided to grant you a hollow victory." Easy suddenly seemed befuddled as to what was actually happening.

Tulsa's Black Wall Street

A story of Greenwood Oklahoma

Then Kenneth Sr. asked Easy, "In what world could a nigger outsmart a white man. Right now I have no more patience for you and your weak plan. Now, if you'll excuse me for a minute." Kenneth Sr. looked around briefly then shouted, "Albert, you out there?" Easy then heard a distant, "Right here Ken," said a man hiding in the trees. Refusing to take his eye off of Kenneth Sr., Easy could hear the footsteps of someone coming up from behind walking toward them.

Easy stood there stoney faced but his heart was beating as if it would burst. About that time, out of the corner of his eye, Easy could see it was Deputy Letchworth, with rifle in hand. With a grin spread over his face showing his crooked, nicotine-stained and rotting teeth Kenneth Sr. said with confidence, "That lummox son of mine did you a disservice. He should have warned you that I don't play fair. Playing fair was for idiots. Boy, I think you just might be outnumbered and in a heap of trouble. What's the matter boy, you ain't got nothing to say? I done killed hundreds of niggers like you who thought they were smarter than me. You just one more that I get to add to my list."

Tulsa's Black Wall Street
A story of Greenwood Oklahoma

As Kenneth Sr. and Deputy Letchworth stood there in silence eyeing him down, Easy did not utter a single word. There was complete silence as Easy glanced around nervously before closing his eyes. Easy prayed to God he had not overplayed his hand. Suddenly, three rifle shots rang out, breaking the silence.

Tulsa's Black Wall Street
A story of Greenwood Oklahoma

Chapter 17

As if grabbed by an unseen hand and twirled violently around before being released, Deputy Letchworth was forcefully spun to the ground. He flopped to the ground trembling, convulsing and screaming like a wounded animal. Blood flowed freely from the two gaping holes in his body. Kenneth Sr. wore a puzzled expression. Only a moment ago he was on the verge of vanquishing the proverbial pebble in his shoe, but now it appeared the situation had reversed dramatically. Suddenly he found himself in unfamiliar terrain and there were more questions than answers.

Still holding the shotgun, Easy shouted out, "Damn Willie, you had me worried." Walking from the tree line behind Kenneth Sr. Willie said, "A rifle is not my weapon of choice brother. I haven't used a rifle since the war and I did not want to hit you." Then strolling up to Deputy Letchworth, he asked "You still living snowflake?" The Deputy's breathing came in ragged, shallow gasps and he was drooling blood. He tried to talk but his response was lost in an involuntary sob. "Let me help you out," Willie responded while pulling out a pistol.

Tulsa's Black Wall Street
A story of Greenwood Oklahoma

Willie fired two more rounds in the Deputy's head causing a scarlet liquid to squirt. "Damn man he was dying, why shoot him" Easy asked? "He was not dying fast enough for me", Willie retorted. As they encircled Kenneth Sr., Willie asked "Is this the redneck you were waiting for?" Easy responded, "Yes that's him." Without hesitation Willie said, "Well, let's just kill him and go." Kenneth Sr.'s face suddenly fell faster than Wall Street during the Crash of 1929. In that instant his skin turned grey, his mouth hung with his lips slightly parted and his eyes were as wide as they could stretch. He came to the unbelievable realization that he had been outsmarted by this young black man.

Staring at Kenneth Sr. without emotion Easy calmly said, "Did you know that I killed plenty of German's in Europe? Yep, us colored boys fought with the French and they taught us a lot about fighting and strategy. We fought in a unit under this French platoon commander named Lieutenant Faucheux. In planning he would always ask, 'Soldier, what would you do if your first battle plan failed? You must always have a back-up plan.' That is why I had Willie here hiding in the woods. After killing white boys in combat, killing you is no more intimidating that squishing an ant. Jr. did warn me that you didn't play fair and I thank him for that."

Tulsa's Black Wall Street

A story of Greenwood Oklahoma

A paralyzing fear spread through Kenneth Sr.'s body. Starting to hyper-ventilate, he tried to avoid making a sound as sweat drenched his skin. Despite his efforts, Easy spotted the terror in Kenneth Sr.'s eyes. With his enforcer now dead and no mob backing him, the old man was alone and painfully aware of his vulnerability. The prolonged stress on Kenneth Sr. created a sense of being physically and mentally drained. It occurred to Easy that the old man had nothing more to give and was emotionally susceptible. Now was the perfect time to go for the jugular and attack him mentally.

Treating Kenneth Sr. condescendingly Easy said, "Before you leave this world I want you to suffer the way you made poor Isaac Washington suffer. The battering and bruising Rebecca received that night came from your hands not Isaac's. You hung him with the full knowledge that he neither beat nor assaulted your daughter. Well let me tell you about Rebecca and the night she came home late. You sent her on an errand to get some pig medicine. On that night I can promise you she got a lot more than pig medicine." Pointing in the direction of a spot near the creek Easy continued, "I had her over there in those woods grinding her corn. Ken; I hope you don't mind if I call you Ken since me and Rebecca are so close, she was juicier than a fresh water clam.

Tulsa's Black Wall Street
A story of Greenwood Oklahoma

She just couldn't get enough of my Oklahoma black snake. In fact, my friend Willie here had to help me out. She didn't want to leave. Can you imagine that Ken? Can you imagine Rebecca lying there sweating and moaning while enjoying to big black Johnsons? " As Easy tortured him mentally, each second seemed to play on forever, in Kenneth Sr.'s mind. The fear that what Easy had said was possibly true looped around in his mind until there was no room for anything else. Trapped in his own psychosis, a living nightmare for him, Easy had played perfectly on Kenneth Sr.'s deepest fears. Clinching his fists, Kenneth Sr. was sweating even more, the hairs on the nape of his neck bristled and his body began to tremble.

Now in a state of the mind where he had difficulty determining what was real and what was not, Kenneth Sr. started to speak. However, before he could utter a single word Easy plunged his knife deep into Kenneth Sr.'s body. The knife's blade met soft and rotund flesh, making a gratifying squish as the tip sank deep enough to make Kenneth Sr. scream. Easy slowly twisted the blade in his hands, all the while sinking it deeper and deeper into his victim. Easy could hear Kenneth Sr.'s skin tear to shreds and the sound of muscles being gouged as the knife rotated.

Tulsa's Black Wall Street

A story of Greenwood Oklahoma

When Easy pulled the blade out, Kenneth Sr. rolled around the ground with an agonizing howl. As he lay in agony Kenneth Sr.'s blood and guts flooded from his ripped open stomach.

Standing there with Kenneth Sr. dying at his feet, Easy was a bit melancholy. He was thinking of Jr.'s untimely death, the riots in Tulsa and all the black murders associated with this one man. Seeing that he was obviously troubled, Willie placed his hand on Easy's shoulder and said, "That old man got what he deserved." Willie looked down for a moment, pulled his pistol and then fired a bullet into Kenneth Sr.'s head. Willie looked at Easy to say, "A man like that can't be dead enough." A little puzzled Willie asked, "Why did you tell that man we had been with his daughter? There was no truth to none of that." Easy explained, that he wanted Kenneth Sr. to experience the same pain and mental anguish that he had inflicted on all his victims. Easy told Willie that Kenneth Sr. deserved to get a taste of his own medicine. Leering at the recently deceased, Willie responded, "Easy, I agree with you. He should get a taste of his own medicine." Willie walked over and ransacked the old rusty truck finding a can of coal oil. He retrieved the coal oil poured it all over Kenneth Sr.'s body and set it on fire.

Tulsa's Black Wall Street
A story of Greenwood Oklahoma

Switching his attention to the surrounding scenery, Easy said "Well Willie, we have faced a terrible storm the past few days. I must be honest, you do get trigger happy sometime, but you are my boy. You have been there for me through thick and thin. I would say that we have worn out our welcome around here. I love this community and there is sadness in leaving but it's time to go. I have lost almost everything that I had, but all that I have is yours my friend."

With his usual swagger Willie responded, "Easy you have always be straight up with me and treated me like blood. You are my family and always will be. Years down the road people may forget what someone once said to them, people may forget what someone did for them, but people will never forget how a person made them feel. You get me. You are my nigga so, what's money between friends? Besides you don't have a worry about money, I got some cash stashed for us." Easy tilted his head to the side, his face twisted and with a puzzled look he asked, "What did you say?" Savoring the moment, Willie did not answer immediately. He just stood there with a slick smile spreading across his face and devilish mischief lurking in his eyes. "Damn Easy, don't look at me like you didn't hear or understand what I just said.

Tulsa's Black Wall Street

A story of Greenwood Oklahoma

I will always have your back. Like the rug said to the floor, I got you covered. I said I have some cash stashed for us. Let's go get it."

Easy followed Willie as he walked toward Worley's creek. As they walked Willie explained how the Klan's planned distraction on the day they lynched Isaac Washington was brilliant strategy. Willie was amazed that rednecks that stupid could come up with such a good plan. He rationalized that if it worked once then it would work twice. The only thing he needed was the element of surprise. Willie reminded Easy of the multiple fire bombings in Tulsa earlier in the morning. He admitted to engineering those fire bombings. Explosions at the Mayor's home, an oil executive's home and one of Tulsa's banks were strategically targeted. The ensuing fires distracted the Fire Department, National Guard and a huge segment of the residents. A large portion of people had generated into a massive bloodthirsty mob looking to lynch someone. The plan worked perfectly because there was virtually no one protecting downtown Tulsa. Willie told Easy, "There was no one in sight man. Yes sir, I will give credit where credit is due, them white boys had a good strategy. Breaking into and robbing that bank was like taking candy from a baby."

Tulsa's Black Wall Street

A story of Greenwood Oklahoma

When they reached the hiding spot, he looked at Easy with that mischievous "Willie smile" before digging up the loot. Willie quickly counted the money. His plunder from the bank job was $72,000.00. Willie split the money and exuberantly handed Easy his $36,000.00 share. Easy could formulate no thought initially other than to register on his face that he was shocked.

After a few seconds, Easy let out a long breath, like he didn't even know he'd been holding it in and a Cheshire cat like grin appeared on his face. Easy and Willie celebrated their plunder like pirates as they jumped and danced like they'd forgotten how to stand still. Following a brief celebration, Easy commented to his friend, "Well Willie let's break, we've got a lot of road to cover." They quickly gathered their belongings and departed. With the aid of his Uncle Chebona Bula Red Eagle, Easy and Willie escaped Oklahoma through the backroads and trails of the Indian nations.

Tulsa's Black Wall Street
A story of Greenwood Oklahoma

Chapter 18

Between 1921 – 1925 The Greenwood District in Tulsa, Oklahoma, grew into the most famous and prosperous black community in the United States. It was strictly segregated from the rest of Tulsa, but still it flourished. Unfortunately the economic status of this proud community could not save its people from the racial hostility of their day. After a mere twenty four hour period 35 city blocks lay in charred ruins. An estimated 10,000 people were left homeless and over a six thousand buildings were destroyed. The white invasion of Greenwood did not just destroy a community, it killed an economy. The riot was unsympathetically covered nationally by white newspapers and the reported number of deaths varied widely. Because whites used multiple mass graves, to this date an official death toll remain undetermined.

Black residents of Greenwood perceived the violent rampage was started by white racism. The generalized white perception was that blacks were out of line and needed to be put back in their place. White politicians and white media framed the Tulsa riot as an uprising started by lawless blacks.

Tulsa's Black Wall Street

A story of Greenwood Oklahoma

Tulsa newspapers regularly referred to the Greenwood district as "Little Africa" and "nigger town." Blacks were portrayed in the white press as "bad niggers" who drank booze, took dope, and ran around with guns. Generally, white politicians and residents perceived the black community as predisposed to crime and in need of social control. These assumptions of criminality allowed whites to justify their deadly violence. In fact many prominent state and city officials were affiliated with the Ku Klux Klan. These same officials participated in the savagery against Greenwood residents.

Interestingly enough, there were very few criminal charges in the wake of the Greenwood riot. No prosecution took place against any white person for actions committed during the violence. The blame for the destruction was put squarely on the black residents of Greenwood and several were charged. One of the most unfortunate and widely-accepted ideas about historical thinking is that during every clash, combat or warfare, it's the winner that gets the booty. This can be summed up by the phrase from New York Senator William L. Marcy in 1828 "to the victor belong the spoils."

Tulsa's Black Wall Street

A story of Greenwood Oklahoma

Senator Macy was referring to the victory of Andrew Jackson in the election of 1828, with the term spoils meaning goods or benefits taken from the loser in any competition. During a war when two cultures clash, the loser is usually obliterated, and the winner gets to write the history. History as written by winners, tend to glorify their own cause and disparage the conquered foe. The "winners" have the power to shape historical narratives through the news, school textbooks, movies, and a range of other mediums. All these mediums are powerful venues for establishing political ideologies and shaping personal assumptions. In the case of Tulsa, whites exploited their power to achieve their own ends. They also shaped history by putting forth only their version of events in Greenwood. However, Easy was never charged with a crime nor ever heard from again by the white people of Tulsa; except for one special person. For Tulsa residents, it was almost as if he had vanished into thin air. There were a plethora of questions surrounding the murders of Deputy Albert Letchworth, Kenneth Chase Sr., Kenneth Chase Jr. and the bank robbery. However despite their frustrations and suspicions, charges were never filed against anyone.

Despite hundreds of witnesses, Willie was not charged with the murder of a white man.

Tulsa's Black Wall Street
A story of Greenwood Oklahoma

To capture or charge a criminal, a good description of a suspect is vital for law enforcement. In all of the confusion no one could provide an accurate description of Willie. Of approximately 200 interviews the only two items that were consistent in describing Willie was: (1) Male and (2) Negro. Ironically one frustrated witness complained in his interview that he was unable to identify the culprit because "all negroes looked alike." Much like a bad nightmare, state and local officials just wanted the whole thing over with. The city settled into an uneasy peace, and virtual silence about the events of that 24 hour period. As if it never happened, the riot was largely omitted from local and state, as well as national histories.

The following few months after the Greenwood riot Emma Burns, the alleged assault victim, kept mostly to herself. Inconspicuously she quietly went about her daily business keeping mostly to herself. Rumors and gossip swirled about the alleged assault. There were also many questions about the nature of her relationship with Easy. Emma had opened her heart to love without restraint and was genuinely devastated by Easy leaving. A part of her now was no longer whole.

Tulsa's Black Wall Street
A story of Greenwood Oklahoma

Outside of his immediate family, Emma was the only person to know of Easy's whereabouts. Loving Easy had been taboo, but it forever changed her and her views on society. Not wanting to live with regret Emma reasoned the biggest challenge was building the courage to follow her heart. Approximately six months after the Greenwood riot Emma quit her job. Surprising her family, Emma packed up everything she owned and discreetly left town without a forwarding address. Neither her parents, siblings, nor anyone else in Tulsa, ever heard from her or Easy. Ever again.

Printed in Japan
落丁、乱丁本のお問い合わせは
Amazon.co.jp カスタマーサービスへ